"The somber beauty of the *Inferno* brought up to the twentieth century with care and humor and with some sins Dante didn't even suspect."

—Frank Herbert, author of *Dune*

"Intriguing and ingenious . . . a fast, amusing and vivid book, by a writing team noted for intelligence and imagination." —Roger Zelazny, author of *Lord of Light*

"If they don't manage to 'zap' you (as they did me) at least once, then you're probably not living in the twentieth century."

—Thomas N. Scortia, author of *The Glass Inferno*

"*Inferno* is quite literally a cakewalk through hell. . . . I kid you not, Larry Niven and Jerry Pournelle have had the chutzpah to rewrite Dante's *Inferno* as if they were some unholy hybrid of Roger Zelazny, Robert Heinlein, and Philip Jose Farmer. You are right there in the nether-reaches of the ultimate Sam Peckinpah movie with all the matter-of-fact solidity of a Hal Clement novel. It gets to you, it really does, this being lunacy of a transcendent order."

—Norman Spinrad, author of *No Direction Home*

INFERNO
is an original POCKET BOOK edition.

Books by Larry Niven and Jerry Pournelle

Inferno
The Mote in God's Eye

Published by POCKET BOOKS

 *Are there paperbound books you want
but cannot find in your retail stores?*

You can get any title in print in **POCKET BOOK** editions. Simply
send retail price, local sales tax, if any, plus 25¢ (50¢ if you
order two or more books) to cover mailing and handling costs to:

MAIL SERVICE DEPARTMENT
POCKET BOOKS • A Division of Simon & Schuster, Inc.
1 West 39th Street • New York, New York 10018

Please send check or money order. We cannot be responsible
for cash.   *Catalogue sent free on request.*

Titles in this series are also available at discounts in quantity
lots for industrial or sales-promotional use. For details write our
Special Projects Agency: The Benjamin Company, Inc., 485
Madison Avenue, New York, New York 10022.

INFERNO

Larry Niven
and
Jerry Pournelle

PUBLISHED BY POCKET BOOKS NEW YORK

INFERNO

POCKET BOOK edition published May, 1976

This original POCKET BOOK edition is printed from brand-new
plates made from newly set, clear, easy-to-read type.
POCKET BOOK editions are published by
POCKET BOOKS,
a division of Simon & Schuster, Inc.,
A GULF+WESTERN COMPANY
630 Fifth Avenue,
New York, N.Y. 10020.
Trademarks registered in the United States
and other countries.

For Dante Alighieri

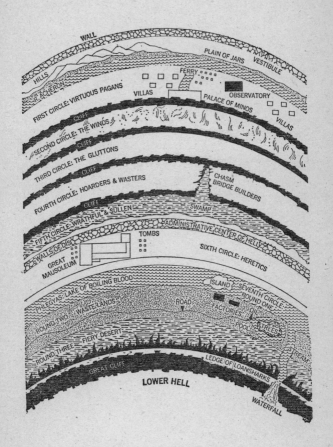

WALL

PLAIN OF JARS

VESTIBULE

HILLS

FERRY

ACHERON

OBSERVATORY

FIRST CIRCLE: VIRTUOUS PAGANS

VILLAS

PALACE OF MINOS

VILLAS

CLIFF

SECOND CIRCLE: THE WINDS

CLIFF

THIRD CIRCLE: THE GLUTTONS

CLIFF

FOURTH CIRCLE: HOARDERS & WASTERS

CHASM
BRIDGE BUILDERS

CLIFF

SWAMP

FIFTH CIRCLE: WRATHFUL & SULLEN

ADMINISTRATIVE CENTER OF HELL

WALLS OF DIS

TOMBS

GREAT
MAUSOLEUM

SIXTH CIRCLE: HERETICS

PHLEGYAS' LAKE OF BOILING BLOOD

ISLAND

SEVENTH CIRCLE

ROUND ONE

ROUND TWO — WASTELANDS

ROAD

FACTORIES

CLIFF

POOL

STREAM

ROUND THREE — FIERY DESERT

GREAT CLIFF

LEDGE OF LOANSHARKS

STREAM

LOWER HELL

WATERFALL

PART I

-||-||-||-||-||-||-||-||-||-||-

1

I THOUGHT ABOUT BEING DEAD.

I could remember every silly detail of that silly last performance. I was dead at the end of it. But how could I think about being dead if I had died?

I thought about that, too, after I stopped having hysterics. There was plenty of time to think.

Call me Allen Carpentier. It's the name I wrote under, and someone will remember it. I was one of the best-known science-fiction writers in the world, and I had a lot of fans. My stories weren't the kind that win awards, but they entertained, and I had written a lot of them. The fans all knew me. Someone ought to remember me.

It was the fans who killed me. At least, they let me do it. It's an old game. At science-fiction conventions the fans try to get their favorite author washed-out stinking drunk. Then they can go home and tell stories about how Allen Carpentier really tied one on and they were right there to see it. They add to the stories until legends are built around what writers do at conventions. It's all in fun. They really like me, and I like them.

I think I do. But the fans vote the Hugo awards, and you have to be popular to win. I'd been nominated five times for awards and never won one, and I was out to make friends that year. Instead of hiding in a back booth with other writers I was at a fan party, drinking with a roomful of short ugly kids with pimples, tall serious Harvard types, girls with long stringy hair, half-pretty girls half-dressed to show it, and damn few people with good manners.

Remember the drinking party in *War and Peace?* Where one of the characters bets he can sit on a window ledge and drink a whole bottle of rum without touching the sides? I made the same bet.

The convention hotel was a big one, and the room was eight stories up. I climbed out and sat with my feet dangling against the smooth stone building. The smog had blown away, and Los Angeles was beautiful. Even with the energy shortage there were lights everywhere, moving rivers of lights on the freeways, blue glows from swimming pools near the hotel, a grid of light stretching out as far as I could see. Somewhere out there were fireworks, but I don't know what they were celebrating.

They handed me the rum. "You're a real sport, Allen," said a middle-aged adolescent. He had acne and halitosis, but he published one of the biggest science-fiction newsletters around. He wouldn't have known a literary reference if it bit him on the nose. "Hey, that's a long way down."

"Right. Beautiful night, isn't it? Arcturus up there, see it? Star with the largest proper motion. Moved a couple of degrees in the last three thousand years. Almost races along."

Carpentier's trivial last words: a meaningless lecture

to people who not only knew it already, but had read it in my own work. I took the rum and tilted my head back to drink.

It was like drinking flaming battery acid. There was no pleasure in it. I'd regret this tomorrow. But the fans began to shout behind me, and that made me feel good until I saw why. Asimov had come in. Asimov wrote science articles and histories and straight novels and commentaries on the Bible and Byron and Shakespeare, and he turned out more material in a year than anyone else writes in a lifetime. I used to steal data and ideas from his columns. The fans were shouting for him, while I risked my neck to give them the biggest performance of all the drunken conventions of Allen Carpentier.

With nobody watching.

The bottle was half empty when my gag reflex cut in and spilled used rum into my nose and sinuses. I jackknifed forward to cough it out of my lungs and pitched right on over.

I don't think anyone saw me fall.

It was an accident, a stupid accident caused by stupid drunkenness, and it was all the fans' fault anyway. They had no business letting me do it! And it was an accident, I know it was. I wasn't feeling *that* sorry for myself.

The city was still alive with lights. A big Roman candle burst with brilliant pinpoints of yellows and greens against the starry skies. The view was pleasant as I floated down the side of the hotel.

It seemed to take a long time to get to the bottom.

2

THE BIG SURPRISE WAS THAT I COULD BE SURPRISED. That I could be anything. That I could be.

I was, but I wasn't. I thought I could see, but there was only a bright uniform metallic color of bronze. Sometimes there were faint sounds, but they didn't mean anything. And when I looked down, I couldn't see myself.

When I tried to move, nothing happened. It felt as if I had moved. My muscles sent the right position signals. But nothing happened, nothing at all.

I couldn't touch anything, not even myself. I couldn't feel anything, or see anything, or sense anything except my own posture. I knew when I was sitting, or standing, or walking, or running, or doubled up like a contortionist, but I felt nothing at all.

I screamed. I could hear the scream, and I shouted for help. Nothing answered.

Dead. I had to be dead. But dead men don't think about death. What do dead men think about? Dead men don't think. I was thinking, but I was dead. That struck me as funny and set off hysterics, and then I'd get myself under control and go round and round with it again.

Dead. This was like nothing any religion had ever taught. Not that I'd ever caught any of the religions going around, but none had warned of this. I certainly wasn't in Heaven, and it was too lonely to be Hell.

It's like this, Carpentier: this is Heaven, but you're the only one who ever made it. Hah!

I couldn't be dead. What, then? Frozen? Frozen! That's it, they've made me a corpsicle! The convention was in Los Angeles, where the frozen-dead movement started and where it has the most supporters. They must have frozen me, put me in a double-walled coffin with liquid nitrogen all around me, and when they tried to revive me the revival didn't work. What am I now? A brain in a bottle, fed by color-coded tubes? Why don't they try to talk to me?

Why don't they kill me?

Maybe they still have hopes of waking me. Hope. Maybe there's hope after all.

It was flattering, at first, to think of teams of specialists working to make me human again. The fans! They'd realized it was their fault, and they'd paid for this! How far in the future would I wake up? What would it be like? Even the definition of *human* might have changed.

Would they have immortality? Stimulation of psychic power centers in the brain? Empires of thousands of worlds? I'd written about all of these, and my books would still be around! I'd be famous. I'd written about—

I'd written stories about future cultures raiding corpsicles for spare parts, transplants. Had that happened to me? My body broken up for spares? Then why was I still alive?

Because they couldn't use my brain.

Then let them throw it out!

Maybe they just couldn't use it yet.

I couldn't tell how long I was there. There was no sense of time passing. I screamed a lot. I ran nowhere forever, to no purpose: I couldn't run out of breath, I never reached a wall. I wrote novels, dozens of them, in my head, with no way to write them down. I relived that last convention party a thousand times. I played games with myself. I remembered every detail of my life, with a brutal honesty I'd never had before; what else could I do? All through it, I was terrified of going mad, and then I'd fight the terror, because that could drive me mad—

I think I did not go mad. But it went on, and on, and on, until I was screaming again.

Get me out of here! Please, anyone, someone, get me out of here!

Nothing happened, of course.

Pull the plug and let me die! Make it stop! Get me out of here!

Nothing.

Hey, Carpentier. Remember "The Chill"? Your hero was a corpsicle, and they'd let his temperature drop too low. His nervous system had become a superconductor. Nobody knew he was alive in there, frozen solid but thinking, screaming in his head, feeling the awful cold—

No! For the love of God, get me out of here!

I was lying on my left side in a field, with dirt under me and warm light all around me. I was staring at my navel, and I could see it! It was the most beautiful sight I'd ever imagined. I was afraid to move; my navel and I might pop like a soap bubble. It took a long time to get the nerve to lift my head.

I could see my hands and feet and the rest of me. When I moved my fingers I could see them wriggle.

There wasn't a thing wrong with me. It was as if I had never fallen eight stories to be smashed into jelly.

I was clothed in a loose white gown partly open down the front. Not very surprising, but where was the hospital? Surely they didn't waken Sleepers in the middle of a field?

They? I couldn't see anyone else. There was a field of dirt, trampled here and there, sloping downhill to become a shiny mud flat. I raised my head, and he was standing behind me. A fat man, tall but dumpy and chunky enough that at first I didn't notice his height. His jaw was massively square and jutted out, the first thing I noticed about his face. He had wide lips and a high forehead, and short, blunt, powerful fingers. He wore a hospital gown something like mine.

He was beautiful. Everything was beautiful. But my navel? *Magnifique!*

"You are well?" he asked.

He spoke with an accent: Mediterranean; Spanish, perhaps, or Italian. He was looking closely at me, and he asked again, "You are well?"

"Yes. I think so. Where am I?"

He shrugged. "Always they ask that question first. Where do you think you are?"

I shook my head and grinned for the pleasure of it. It was pleasure to move, to see myself move, to feel my buttocks press against the dirt and know something would oppose my movements. It was ecstasy to see myself in the bright light around me. I looked up at the sky.

There wasn't any sky.

Okay, there has to be a sky. I know that. But I saw nothing. Thick clouds? But there was no detail to the clouds, just a uniform gray above me. Even in my sensation-starved condition it was ugly.

I was in the middle of a field of dirt that stretched a couple of miles to some low brown hills. There were people on the hills, a lot of them, running after something I couldn't make out. I sat up to scan the horizon.

The hills ran up against a high wall that stretched in both directions as far as I could see. It seemed straight as a mathematician's line, but I sensed the slightest of inward curves just before it vanished into deep gloom. There was something wrong with the perspective, but I can't describe precisely what, just that it didn't seem right.

The hills and the mud flats formed a wide strip between the wall and a fast-moving river of water black as ink. The river was a mile away and didn't seem very wide at that distance. I could see it perfectly, another perceptual distortion because it was too far away for the details I could make out.

Beyond the river were green fields and white Mediterranean villas, walled complexes with the squat classical look to them, some quite large. They weren't arranged in any order, and the effect was very pleasing. I turned back to the wall.

Not very high, I thought. High enough to be trouble climbing, perhaps two or three times my six-foot height. I was hampered by the perspective problem. The nearest point of the wall might have been a mile away or ten, though ten seemed ridiculous.

I took a deep breath and didn't like the smells. Fetid, with an acrid tinge, decay and sickly sweet perfume to cover the smells of death, orange blossoms mingled with hospital smells, all subtle enough that I hadn't noticed them before, but sickening all the same. I won't mention the smells often, but they were always there. Most stinks you get used to and soon don't notice, but this had too much in the blend and the blend changed too often. You'd just get used to one and there'd be another.

Beside me on the ground was a small bronze bottle with a classical beaker shape. I figured it would hold maybe a quart. Except for the man standing above me there wasn't another blessed thing.

"Never mind where I am," I said. "Where have I been? I don't remember passing out. I was screaming, and here I am. Where was I?"

"First you ask where you are. Then where you were. Do you think of nothing else you should say?" He was frowning disapproval, as if he didn't like me at all. So what the hell was he doing here?

Breaking me out of wherever I'd been, of course. "Yeah. Thanks."

"You should thank the One who sent me to you."

"Who was that?"

"You asked Him for help—"

"I don't remember asking anyone for help." But this time I'd heard him pronounce the capital letter. "Yeah. 'For the love of God,' I said. Well?"

The fat meaty lips twitched, and his eyes filled with concern. When he looked at me it wasn't in distaste, but in sympathy. "Very well. You will have a great deal to learn. First, I answer your questions. Where are you? You are dead, and you lie on the ground of the Vestibule to Hell. Where were you?" He kicked the bronze bottle with a sandaled foot. "In there."

Hot diggity damn, I'm in the nut hatch and the head loony's come to talk to me.

Carpentier wakes up a thousand years after his last flight and sloppy landing, and already he's in trouble. Spoons and forks and chopsticks, traffic lights, the way a man puts his pants on, all may have to be relearned.

Law and customs change in a thousand years. Society may not even recognize Carpentier as sane.

But wake him in a thirtieth-century loony bin among thirtieth-century twitchies, and now what? How can he adjust to anything?

There were other bottles sitting unattended on the dirt, some larger than mine, some smaller. I don't know why I hadn't noticed them before. I picked one up and dropped it quick. It burned my fingers, and there were faint sounds coming from inside it.

It sounded like human speech in a foreign language, a voice screaming curses. That tone couldn't be anything else. Endless curses screamed—

Why would they put radios in old bronze bottles and scatter them through the loony bin? My hypothesis needed more work.

The people up on the hills were still running. They'd looped back to about where I'd first seen them, and whatever it was they chased, they hadn't caught it yet. Do they let the nuts run in circles in futuristic loony bins?

Where had I been? Where? There wasn't any hospital around here, no facilities for keeping all or part of a corpsicle, nothing but this crazy man and a lot of bronze bottles and people running in circles and—and insects of some kind. Something whined and did a kamikaze into my ear. Something else stung me on the back of the neck. I slapped frantically, but there wasn't anything to see.

It felt good even to hurt myself slapping.

My "rescuer" was patiently waiting for me to make some response. It wouldn't hurt to humor him until I had more information.

"Okay, I'm in the Vestibule of Hell and I was in a bottle. A djinn bottle. How long?" I told him the date on which I'd fallen from the window.

He shrugged. "You will find that time has not the same meaning here as you are accustomed to. We have all the time we will ever need. Eternity lies before us. I am unable to tell you how long you were in that beaker, but I can assure you it is not important."

Not important? I almost went mad in there! The realization made me start to shiver, and he dropped to his knees beside me, all concern, to put a hand on my shoulder.

"It is over now. God will not allow you back into the bottle. I cannot assure you that there will be nothing worse before you leave Hell. There will be much worse. But with faith and hope you will endure it, and you will be able to leave."

"That's a lot of comfort."

"It is infinite comfort. Did you not understand? I know a way out of here!"

"Yeah? So do I. Right over that wall."

He laughed. I listened for a while, and it got irritating. Finally he choked it down to a chuckle. "I'm sorry, but they all say that, too. I suppose there is nothing for it but to let you try. After all—we have plenty of time." He laughed again.

Now what? Would he turn me in if I tried to climb the wall? I got up, surprised at how good I felt except for the gnats and the smell. My imaginary exercises in the bottle—

Look, wherever I really spent all that time, effectively I was in a bottle, right? It's a convenient figure of speech. Anyway, my exercises in the bottle had paid off. I started briskly toward the wall.

Wherever the ground dipped low it became squishy mud, ankle-deep, with small live things in it. I tried to stick to the high ground. The fat man kept right alongside me. There was no chucking him. After a while I said, "If we're going to walk together I might as well know your name."

"Benito. Call me Benny if you like."

"Okay. Benito." *Benny* sounded much too friendly. "Look, Benito, don't you want out of here?"

I hit a nerve. He stopped short, his wide face a gamut of emotions unlike anything I'd even seen. After a long time he said, "Yes."

"Then come over the wall with me."

"I can't. You can't. You'll see." He wouldn't say anything else, just kept pace with me as I walked on.

And on.

And on, and on, and on. The wall was a *long* way off. I was right about the perspective. We'd been walking for over an hour as far as I could tell, and the wall looked no closer.

We walked until we were exhausted, and it was still a long way off. I sat down in the mud to slap gnats. "Didn't seem that far. How high is that thing, anyway? Must be colossal."

"It is no more than three meters high."

"Don't be silly."

"Look behind you."

That was the shock of my life. The river was now maybe three miles away instead of one. And we'd walked for *hours*. But—

Benito nodded. "We could walk for eternity and never reach the wall. And we *have* eternity. No, you don't believe me. Very well, convince yourself. Continue toward the wall. Continue until even you are certain it can never be reached, and then I will tell you how you can escape."

It took me several hours, but I finally believed him.

The wall was like light speed. We could get arbitrarily close, but we couldn't ever reach it. Like light speed, or the bottom of a black hole, but like nothing else in the universe I knew.

We weren't going out this way.

And—and just where were we?

3

I SAT IN THE DIRT AND SLAPPED GNATS WHILE BENITO explained it again.

"We are dead and in Hell. This is the Vestibule to Hell, where those who would make no choices in life are condemned. Neither warm nor cold, believers nor blasphemers—you see them in the hills. They chase a banner they will never catch."

I remembered then. "Dante's *Inferno?*"

Benito nodded, his big square jaw heaving like a broaching whale. "You have read the *Inferno,* then. Good. That was the first clue I had to the way out of here. We must go down—"

"Sure, all the way." Something about a lake of ice, and a hole in the center of it. It had been a long time since I had read Dante. I couldn't see that remembering a thirteenth-century book would do me any good to begin with. This couldn't possibly be the real Hell. Dante's cosmology had been ludicrous, for one thing.

So where was I? "How come you're so sure this is the place Dante described?"

"Where else could it be? All of the features are here. All of the details."

And I'd been dead a long time. Centuries? What kind of civilization would build an exact copy of Dante's Inferno? An Infernoland. Was it part of a larger amusement park, like Frontierland in the Disneyland complex? Or was Infernoland all there was to it?

Who was Benito? A stooge, or a revived corpsicle like me?

The wall. How had they managed that trick? The wall hadn't moved, and I certainly had. Some kind of local field effect? A time slip? Bent space? Come on, Carpentier, you *wrote* the stuff. What's the explanation? Not *the* way they did it, just a plausible way!

"First, we must cross the river," Benito was saying. "Do you believe me now when I tell you that you must not attempt to swim it, or even get wet from it, or must you try that too?"

"What happens if I just dive in?"

"Then you will be as you were in the bottle. Aware and unable to move. But it will be very cold, and very uncomfortable, and you will be there for all eternity knowing you put yourself there."

I shuddered and slapped a gnat. He might be lying. I wasn't going to try it.

It looked very nice across the river, and that was where we had to get before we could find Dante Alighieri's escape hole in the center of Infernoland. The hell with getting to the center! Let me get to those villas over there and I'd be happy enough. "Who's on the other side of the river?"

"Virtuous pagans," Benito answered. "Those who never knew the Word of God, but kept the Commandments. They are not persecuted. Their fate may be the most cruel of all those in this place."

"Because they aren't tortured?"

"Because they think they are happy. You'll find out, let us go and see them."

"How?"

"There is a ferryboat. Once it was a rowing boat, but—"

"Got overcrowded in Hell. Too many arrivals. Sure." And in Disneyland I'd been on a Mississippi riverboat big enough for fifty or sixty people to walk around on. It chugged around on a little pond it shared with a miniature clipper ship. The Builders of Infernoland had a sense of humor, putting a ferryboat in place of Charon's old rowboat.

Maybe we'd meet some of the paying customers on the ferry. I didn't think Benito was one. He behaved more like a fanatical Catholic.

And what was I? Nobody had given me any role to play. Who inhabits Infernoland?

Who inhabits the Inferno?

Damned souls. Could that be my job now—to play damned soul for the amusement of tourists? It wasn't a role I liked very much.

It took as long to leave the wall as it had to go toward it. At least things were consistent. There were laws to this place, if only I could discover them.

When we passed the bottle that had been beside me when I woke up, we turned left and angled toward the river. An old drinking song from science-fiction conventions kept running through my head. "If hosen and shoon thou never gavest men, *every night and all,* the fire will burn thee to the bare bone, *and Christ receive thy soul.*" Was that really where I was, in a real Hell, where justice was meted out to the ungodly?

Scary. It would mean that there was a real God, and maybe Jonah was swallowed by a whale in the

Mediterranean Sea, and Joshua ben Nun really did stop the Earth's rotation for trivial purposes . . .

There was something leaning against a rock. At first I couldn't make it out: a pink mound with hair trailing down one side. We got closer and the mound became five-hundred-odd pounds of woman sitting cross-legged in stinking mud. A swarm of gnats hummed around her. She didn't bother to swat them.

She looked up at us with lifeless eyes. Benito took my arm to hurry me on past her, but I shook him off. She couldn't be quite sane either, but she might be able to tell me something straight. It was more than he would do, and I needed help.

I squatted down to look into her face. She was pathetic, hardly in shape to help anyone, including herself. Far back within tunnels of fat were tiny sparks of life, dull gray against black. Hopeless eyes, almost lifeless.

Her voice was a husky whisper. "Well?"

"I don't know where I am. I just got here, and I have to know. Can you help me?"

"Help *you!* I died, and then *this* happened to me!"

"Died?"

"How else do you get into Hell?" Her voice rose to demand attention despite my shocked surprise. The full force of her breath washed over in waves. "What did I do? I don't *deserve* this! I don't belong here *at all,*" she wailed. "I was beautiful. I could eat like a horse and burn it off in an hour. Then I woke up here, like *this!*" Her voice dropped to a low, confidential murmur. "We're in the hands of infinite power and infinite sadism."

I shied back. Another one.

"Is there nothing you can do?" Benito asked her.

"Sure. I can chase banners to keep slim. What's

the point of that? They won't let you do anything meaningful."

I shuddered. It could have been me. "Why would anyone do this to you?"

"I . . . think it must have been because ten-million fat people were cursing me." Her voice turned venomous. "Fat, fat, fat people with no willpower and no self-respect."

"Why?"

"For doing my job! For trying to help people, trying to save them from themselves! For banning cyclamates, that's why! It was for their own good," she ranted. "You can't trust people to be moderate about anything. Some people get sick on cyclamates. They have to be helped. And this is what I get for helping them!"

"We're trying to escape. Want to come with us? Benito thinks we can get out by going down to the center of this crazy place."

A little spark of interest flared in her eyes, and I held my breath. My open mouth had sent me floating down the side of a building; when would I learn to keep it closed? If she came with us we'd never get away. What good was she?

She struggled to get up, then collapsed against her rock. "No, thank you."

"Right." I started to say something else in parting, but what? If anything went at all right, I'd never see her again. I just walked away, and she let her head slump back into the mounds of fat that bulged at her neck.

As we walked away, Benito asked, "What are cyclamates?"

I slapped at a gnat. The gnats were everywhere, stinging us both, but Benito didn't bother to slap at them. "Sugar substitute. For people who want to lose weight."

He frowned. "If there is too much to eat, surely it would be better to eat less and share with those who have none."

I looked at his big paunch and said nothing.

"I too am in Hell," he reminded me.

"Ah. And they can do what they did to her to you . . ." I shuddered. We were lucky.

"I take it you did not agree with her policy?"

"Idiots. If they'd fed as much sugar to the control rats as they gave cyclamates to the experimental group, they'd have killed the controls first. Instead, they doomed a lot of people to fat. There wasn't a good substitute for cyclamates. I know one guy who bought up cases and cases of a cyclamate diet drink just before the ban hit. He used to give cases of 'vintage Tab' as Christmas presents. They were appreciated, too."

Benito said nothing.

"I know a couple who used to drive up to Canada every so often just to buy cyclamates. It was a *stupid* policy." I looked back over my shoulder at the shapeless pink mound. "Still, it seems a little extreme, what they did to her."

"It is not just?"

"How can you call that *just?*" I didn't say anything else, but I remembered what she'd said. " 'We're in the hands of infinite power and infinite sadism.' "

And just who in Hell was Benito? A paying customer having sport? A damned soul like me? Or one of the paid crew of Infernoland? He talked like a religious fanatic; he seemed to take everything at face value.

Did I dare follow him? But what else could I do? One thing was certain: if he could think that woman had been treated justly, he was not much better than a devil himself.

Hey, Carpentier. Would an artificial Hell have artificial devils? I looked at Benito more closely. He was partly bald. There were no horns on his forehead.

We seemed to be covering a lot of ground, as if the effect of too much distance to the wall had been played in reverse. Suddenly we were part of a crowd, all streaming toward the river. Nobody was pushing them along, but they didn't seem friendly and they didn't talk among themselves. Each one was huddled in toward himself, not looking where he was going. Or she, there were a lot of women.

The ferryboat captain had a long white beard and eyes like burning coals. He screamed in rage when anyone was slow getting aboard. We were pressed together on deck, a mass of us so tightly packed that we couldn't move.

"You again!" He'd turned his burning eyes on Benito. "You've come here before! Well, you won't escape again!" He swung a long billyclub at Benito. It hit with a crack that I thought would break my guide's skull, but it only staggered him.

More people packed the decks until I couldn't even see. Finally I felt the boat begin to move. By then I'd have been glad to stay behind, but there was no way off the boat.

Two voices whispered intensely near my ear:

"Why didn't you stop when I screamed?"

"Because you *startled* me into taking my *foot* off the brake. At least I'll never have to listen to your backseat driving again—"

"But we're in Hell, darling. They'll probably put us in a car with no brakes. Maybe they'll give you a horn. You'll like that."

"Shut up! Shut up!"

She did, and quiet descended. No crowd is that quiet. It was as if nobody had anything to say to anyone.

We bumped solid ground. "All off," Charon shouted. "Damned souls! Damned forever! You cursed God, and now you'll pay for it!"

"Damn God and everyone else!" "Piss on you!" "Up the people!" "You're mucking bastards, all of you, get off my *foot!*" "But I don't *belong* here." "What'd I do? Just tell me—" "Damn the lot of you, I died a *man!*"

We pushed and shoved and danced to keep our feet in the swarm. At least we were on the other side. The crowd was hurrying downhill, along a road that ran between thick, high walls. I hung back, hoping Benito would go with the rest. No such luck. The road turned and twisted so we couldn't see what was ahead, but that was good because after a while we were alone.

I tried to climb the wall. It was a tough scramble, and I kept falling back. After the fourth time I sat there below the wall and whimpered.

"Would you like help?" Benito asked.

"Sure. I thought you said the only way out was downhill."

"It is, but we have time to explore. Try again, I will lift you."

He practically threw me over the wall. He didn't look that strong. I sat on top for a second and looked down at him. He seemed to be waiting for me to help him up.

And now what, Carpentier? Fair's fair, he helped you. Yeah, but why? Leave him behind, he's trouble.

But he knows things I don't. And he got me out of the bottle.

Did he? He says he poured you out of a bottle the size of a fifth of rum! Leave him.

I didn't get the chance to decide. While I was thinking it over, Benito began climbing like an alpiner, using tiny cracks and bumps I could hardly see. Pretty soon he got one hand on top of the wall and pulled himself up. He wasn't breathing hard, and he didn't say anything about my sitting there and watching instead of helping.

I turned to look at the countryside. After all, this Infernoland seemed to be modeled on Dante's. A quarter of a century ago the *Inferno* had been a required book for a course in Comparative World Literature. I'd paid as little attention to the book as I could get away with. I remembered almost nothing, but certainly the place had not been pleasant. God's own torture chamber, very medieval.

Vague images came back to me now: devils with pitchforks, trees that talked and bled, giants and centaurs, fire, snakes . . . but were those from the authentic Inferno, or were they hangovers from Oz books and Disney cartoons? *Never mind, Carpentier. You're not going any further.*

4

IT WAS LOVELY ON THE OTHER SIDE OF THE WALL. I
jumped down onto firm ground, grassy and pleasant.
The air was clean, as at the top of a mountain, with
that fresh smell you get only after a hard backpack
into remote country. The gnats were gone. We walked
toward the villas, lovely things, square-built, the colors
of stone by twilight.

There were crowds around us. Men and women
and children—a lot of children, far too many, all
watching us with big round eyes (or almond eyes, Hell
was thoroughly integrated). Adults and children alike
were curious, but none of them said anything.

They didn't want to be near us, either. They shrank
away as we approached.

It was embarrassing. I thought we must be carrying
the smells of the Vestibule area, the fetid stench of
roses and decay. We'd have to find a place to wash.

"I think I'm going to like it here," I said.

Benito looked at me curiously, but he only said,
"Pleasant, isn't it? Here there is no punishment."

The word grated. *Punishment* implies authority,

someone with more power and a moral position superior to yours. I couldn't accept that. We were in the hands of the Builders of Infernoland, and I'd learned all about their moral position on the other side of the black river.

But I didn't flare up at Benito. Lightly I asked, "These, then, are the privileged customers of Hell?"

"Yes." Benito did not smile. "They never sinned. They would have reached Heaven if they had known the Church."

"And the children?"

"Unbaptized."

I'd heard that about Catholic beliefs. Even in Infernoland it seemed a little rough on the kids. "I thought they got Limbo."

"Call it Limbo if you wish. This is the First Circle of Hell." He paused, uncertain. "There are legends that say the children will be born again."

There were as many children here as there were adults! As if the Builders had gotten a discount for quantity. Hmmm. Could these creatures be androids?

It could have come down to a matter of economics. Android infants would be cheaper than android adults: smaller, fewer reflexes. Would it be cheaper to build androids than to find and capture human beings? I couldn't know, not without knowing the source: who the Builders were or why *I* was here—placed here without my consent or knowledge, by an unknown hand. If me, then why not a thousand others? A billion?

Benito wouldn't be much help. He didn't seem to question anything he saw.

Robot or human, child or adult, they didn't seem unhappy. Except those near us . . . "Benito, what's the matter with them?"

"They sense that we do not belong here. I come

from deeper in Hell, and the smell of the depths is on my soul."

"But I don't."

His smile was grim. "They will not accept you either."

I wasn't so sure of that. If I found a way to clean up, and different clothing . . . hmm. Knock someone on the head, steal his toga; why not? Well, partly because they'd tear me apart if they caught me. And partly because there was no privacy here. The villas, maybe. Or—

I pointed upslope toward what might have been a domed planetarium, the nearest building in sight of us. "What's that?"

He looked. "I have never seen it before."

"Come on."

He came, but reluctantly. "We might not be permitted entry. This is a public building, but we are not of the appropriate public."

"We—" I stopped because a white-bearded patriarch swathed in purple-bordered white bedsheets had grasped me roughly by the arm. He asked a rude question in gibberish.

"Go peddle your papers," I informed him.

He frowned. "Recent English? I asked of you why you invade a place not meant for you."

"I'm taking a survey. Are you happy here? Do the arrangements satisfy you?"

He snorted. "No."

"Then," asked Benito, "why not leave? There is a way out."

The bearded man looked him over, while several passersby stopped to listen. He said, "In what direction does it lie?"

"Downslope. One must travel all the way to the center. To know evil is one path to knowing good."

It was lousy dialogue. The bearded man thought so too. "I do not question your knowledge of the depths of Hell," he said pointedly. "I think you lie."

"Why would I? We plan to leave Hell—" Benito was interrupted by raucous laughter. A crowd was gathering, and it wasn't friendly.

"You can all leave." Benito seemed deadly serious. "Come with me, deeper and deeper into Hell. Learn to hate evil—"

"Hatred for salvation?" one of the oldsters asked. "A curious route to salvation."

Benito seemed to know him. "Yet, Epictatus, that is what you must learn. Not to hate men, but to hate their sins. And *that* you cannot do moderately. You *know* the truth, now. You know that reason alone is not enough. You must ask for grace . . ."

I slipped out during the sermon. They were standing there politely waiting for him to finish. What might have been a mob scene had become a formal debate.

How long would that last? Benito was pushing them in a direction they wouldn't even consider, and they didn't like him at all. They'd looked at me the same way; candid contempt, and the high bitter flavor of mockery. They wanted out, and they didn't believe there was any way out, and they were damned well not going to listen long to a man they thought didn't belong with them.

Benito was preaching hatred, and they hated *him*. He should have had more sense. Like me.

The dome: it couldn't be a planetarium. There was no sky here. Conceivably it was a bathhouse where I could wash off the stench and possibly find an unguarded toga. I climbed toward it.

There were no guards. I walked between Doric pillars, up black marble steps to an expanse of black marble floor. Half a dozen people were talking in a circle. They seemed lost in distance, but as far away as I was, when they caught sight of me they turned their backs firmly and continued talking.

The language wasn't familiar at all.

The place was as empty as anything I'd seen since I left the area of the bottles. Six rude sons of bitches, and a thing in the center of the black marble floor. It might have been a sculpture, it might have been a machine. A thick silver ring twelve feet tall, standing on edge, and a control board at its base.

The console looked operational. There were labels, in English. A switch (marked ON, OFF), a joystick, and a notch with a knob in it. The notch ran the whole length of the console.

I tried the joystick. It went in all six directions: left, right, forward, back, push down, pull up. When I used the switch the space within the ring clouded, then became starry space.

It *was* a planetarium.

When I pushed on the joystick nothing happened.

I took a closer look at the markings along the notch. They were logarithmic, labeled in parsecs/second. The knob was all the way to the left.

I moved it hard right and tried the joystick again.

The universe came up and hit me in the face. Whoosh! Stars shot past and around me; a sun came at me and exploded into a fraction of a second of intolerable brightness and was gone. And I was flat on my back a couple of yards from the console.

That was some planetarium!

The half-a-dozen natives were watching me with some amusement. Screw 'em. I went back to the console, moved the knob down to one parsec/second, then to a tenth of that. Tried the joystick.

This time the motion was just obvious. I steered

toward a blue-white star; moved the knob to slow as I approached it. Moved into it.

The brightness should have burned my eyes out. It wasn't even painful. Odd . . .

I went through the center of the star (X-ray blue) and came out the other side (tremendous prominences leaping out ahead of me) and into space. What now? Find a planet? A different star? Stars were easier to find in this sparkling emptiness, but I'd *love* to dive into an Earthlike world. To search out the layers of it, to see the glowing nickel-iron heart. Let's see, that not-too-brilliant white fleck could be a yellow dwarf. I moved the knob—

A large hand fell heavily on my shoulder.

I twitched like a man electrocuted. I turned, and there was the mob scene I thought I'd left behind me: fifty-odd large, heavy men surrounding me and Benito and the Anywhere Machine.

The white-bearded man who spoke English said, "You are leaving."

I said, "Dammit! Why? Nobody else is using the damn machine. I've waited all my life for something like this!"

"We do not want you here," he said. "We waited because we hoped a messenger of the gods would come to remove you. We might have asked him questions . . . but we have tolerated you too long. As for the machine—" One side of his mouth twitched upward. "If you can carry it you may take it with you."

I cursed him. I stopped when his wide-shouldered friends converged. Several of them wore armor! They moved away in a tight circle with Benito and me in the center.

I whispered, "Benito, can't you stop them?"

He looked at me. "How?"

Yeah.

But if I'd known what waited below, I'd have fought them.

5

EVEN WHILE THEY MARCHED US TOWARD THE WALL, Benito never gave up.

"You may leave this place!" he shouted. "Hector! Aeneas! You are not cowards, to stay where it is pleasant when there is everything to gain elsewhere! Come with us!"

They ignored him.

They were compact and tough inside their armor: too tough to fight, even if they were men, which I doubted. *Hector, Aeneas:* I knew the names. I remembered the Abe Lincoln robot at Disneyland. Could the armor be part of them? With inspection plates—

"Where is Vergil?" Benito raved. "He is no longer here, is he? And the Emperor Trajan?"

"We had our chance," said the taller, broader one. "We didn't take it. There will be no other."

"Have none come here since?" Benito demanded.

The soldiers barked bitter laughter. "Many."

"Is it reasonable to suppose that they will never have the opportunity to leave?"

We had come to the wall. "We'll think about it," one said. "Now out with you. Go where you belong." The gate slammed shut behind us.

I went for the wall on the other side. I examined it without joy. The footholds Benito had used would better have fitted a spider.

Benito watched with a wry smile. "You never give up, do you?"

"No."

"Perseverance is commendable. You will need it, but you must develop other virtues, such as prudence. What will happen if you enter the First Circle again?"

"Maybe they won't catch us this time. I won't go near anyone until I've changed clothes and taken a bath."

"Do not tempt the angels," Benito said. He was quite serious. Yeah, and why not? I was expecting devils in Infernoland. Why not angels?

"That messenger they hoped to see. They *wanted* him to come."

"*They* did, yes. But we are fugitives, Allen."

There were no handholds. This time Benito wouldn't help. I was still trying to climb the wall when a flash flood of people spilled into the far end of the alley. As they foamed toward us in dreadful silence I made one last attempt to go up the wall. Then they swept us up and floated us away.

We were in a marble palace. It was enormous, without furniture. The walls were covered with frescoes of bulls and dolphins and pretty girls wearing flounced skirts and little jackets that opened in front to show bare breasts. The palace was lit with torches in bronze holders along the walls, and there wasn't any sign of modern technology at all.

Except for the palace itself. It wound on and on, chamber after chamber, huge staircases with great pillars inscribed in languages I couldn't read. It was too big; it must have been prestressed concrete or something better. I would have liked to stay and look around, but we were embedded in the flow of the crowd. Nobody spoke or paid us any attention. I was glad for Benito's company. Crowds of strangers bug me, and this one was worse than New York commuters, everyone wrapped up in himself.

We spilled into an enormous room open at the far end. I had a good view through the pillars. The ground sloped sharply away into the bleakest landscape I'd ever seen. The castle was perched on the side of an enormous bowl, a world-sized bowl. Far down into it were the glimmers of fires and the shadow of smoke. I couldn't see far into the smog that hung over everything.

There was a throne at the far end of the audience chamber. An alien occupied it. He was vaguely bovine, but I'd have taken him for an oversized man if it hadn't been for his tail.

Tail!

"What *is* that?" I demanded.

"Minos. Judge of the Dead," said Benito.

The Builders had mixed some Egyptian or Cretan mythology with their Christianity. That, or they'd had to warp their landscape to fit a genuine alien. I could believe a cropping beast becoming an intelligent biped, given time and impetus and perhaps an assist from biological engineers. I'd written stories about that kind of thing.

Could Minos be one of the Builders?

People went up to present themselves to the monster. I couldn't hear what the girl in the yellow dress was telling it, but it grinned and nodded. Abruptly its tail looped out and wrapped around and around the girl. It lifted her.

The tail stretched like the limbs of Plastic Man in the old comic books. The girl shot between two pillars and dwindled, dwindled, dwindled to a speck. Minos' tail must have been tens of miles long at that point. It came snaking back through the air, while the speck that was the girl sank like a single snowflake.

My willing suspension of disbelief went all to hell. I started to giggle hysterically.

Nobody noticed. Nobody but Benito, who watched curiously as I gathered the shreds of my self-control, took him by the arm, pointed at "Minos" and said, "He can't *do* that!"

He was doing it again! The tail stretched out between the pillars like an infinite length of snake, dropped a man in a postman's uniform into the murky air, and came coiling back.

But there wasn't room! Even ignoring the moment arm—that much weight at the end of that much length should have toppled him, and how could such a length of tail, *flexible* tail, be strong enough to stay almost straight? But ignore that, and tell me where there was room for tens of miles of tail to be coiled inside his body?

His feet weren't anchored; I watched until I saw them both move. The tail wasn't stored in the floor, then.

"Are you all right?" Benito asked.

My vision was graying out; my whole body had

a buzzing foot's-asleep feeling. I said, "I'm going to faint."

"You can't faint here. Hold fast." His hand gripped my shoulder.

A dark-haired woman, quite pretty, was encoiled in the tail until she nearly vanished, lifted, and sent spinning off down the bowl. A man in a cabbie's uniform was next. Three loops of tail and out he went into space. And another, and another—

There were thousands here. We'd starve before we reached our turn.

But I didn't feel hungry, and hadn't felt hungry since I left the bottle, and that was hours ago. Also, something was wrong with time. "Minos" was in no hurry. Quite the opposite. He took plenty of time to deal with each case, and there were plenty of cases; yet the crowd thinned out much faster than it should have.

Where were they going? I never saw anyone leave the room, but there had to be other audience chambers, people slipping off into side passages. There must have been hundreds, perhaps thousands, of copies of "Minos."

Ridiculous mummery. But the tail, Carpentier! Hidden in hyperspace, or snaking out of an alternate time track? If the Builders have that kind of technology, how long were you dead? Ten thousand years? A million?

It was our turn. We approached together. Not many had come up in pairs.

"Sodomites, huh?" Minos said. "Seventh Circle, Third Level. Or have you got something worse to confess?"

I said, "I refuse to answer on grounds that my—"

He looked a lot like an angry bull when he frowned, and nothing at all like a machine. He turned to Benito. "You've been here before. Why have you left your proper place?"

"Is that your affair? You see I roam freely through Hell."

"Yes. How?"

"It has been willed that I may do so. You have no right to interfere."

Minos waved at me. "And this one?"

"He has come from the Vestibule," Benito said. "You will note that he comes of his own accord. You may not judge him."

"Lawyers." Minos laughed. "I have problems with lawyers. There are so *many* places appropriate to that breed. Where are you two going, then?"

"Down."

"Back to the First Circle."

We'd spoken simultaneously. Minos laughed. "Back you will not go. Are you sure you don't want me to judge you, Allen Carpenter? My judgment is just and fair. You could choose worse for yourself than justice."

"Cease!" Benito commanded. I jumped. He was a changed man. Power seemed to gather around him as he struck a pose, massive chin jutting out in defiance, his face both calm and stern. Once upon a time he had been used to obedience.

"I am permitted to judge . . ." Suddenly Minos sounded petulant.

"You have already judged me. What other power have you? And this man is not under your jurisdiction. Leave us alone to go in peace."

"Not back up."

"No. Down."

Minos laughed. He waved toward the steps leading

down into the bowl from his throne. "Depart. Thou art sent!" He was still laughing as we started down those steps, the mocking laughter in our ears until we lost sight of the palace.

6

WE WERE ALL RIGHT AS LONG AS THE STEPS CON-
tinued. Unfortunately they soon trailed away into a
broken slope that still dropped at forty-five degrees
or so. At the same time a wind began to rise. Benito
and I turned to face the slope and backed down on
toes and knees and hands.

In fact, the hurricane in my head (Where does
the Minos-thing keep its tail? What is Benito, that he
gives orders to an inhuman that judges all others
who come before it? Is this Hell for a science-fiction
writer, where physical laws are whimsical and puzzles
have no answers?) was nothing compared to the hurricane we were backing into. We moved flat against the
slope, clutching at the rock and digging into the dirt
for footholds.

Benito yelled, "Minos called you Carpenter. Not
Carpentier."

I'd been wondering how the monster knew. "I was
born Carpenter," I shouted down at Benito. "I added

45

the 'i' to make the name more interesting, easier to
remember. I wrote under Carpentier." And when I
talked to myself (I didn't add) it was Carpentier I
talked to. I'd started that in an effort to memorize
the new pronunciation.

We'd backed onto a broad ledge. I stayed flat as
I looked around.

Someone was dancing to the music of the howling
wind.

He was bones and paunch and long flying hair just
graying unevenly at the temples. He jumped and
danced and flapped his arms like a bird, grim deter-
mination on his homely face.

I hollered into the wind. "Hey, friend—"

He didn't wait for the question. "If I could just
get off the ground!" he wailed. "The guy in the
helmet's got a *dozen!*"

Hey, yeah, I'd been right the first time! It was a
futuristic loony bin geared for psychodrama on the
grand scale! Let them work out their delusions here,
and maybe they'd be fit for whatever unimaginable
society they'd flunked out of . . . And I had answers
to all the questions, in that wonderful moment before
I followed his eyes upward.

The air was full of flying people.

They weren't exactly guiding their flight. The wind
had them. Here it churned them in a momentary
funnel, then flung them outward. There they came in
a straight blast; it hit a shoulder of the mountain and
churned the trapped beings into eddy currents. The
people flew like Kleenex in a hurricane, but they
looked like people, and they howled like Kansans
caught outside in a flash tornado.

Most of them were flying in man-and-woman pairs.
But, yeah, there was one guy surrounded by a good

dozen girls, all in a whirling clump at the top of a rising air column.

The bony guy on the ledge ran off flapping his arms. There were others along the base, men and women, all trying to fly. I had different ideas. I gripped the rock hard and stayed flat.

"The Carnal," Benito screamed into the wind. "Those who warped all that mattered in their lives for lust. I imagine those at the base of the cliff were unsuccessful lovers. We will be in less danger on the next ledge." He started crawling.

"Benito! That's it!" I cried. "We'll fly out of here!"

He turned in astonishment. It was a mistake. The wind slipped under his raised shoulders and lifted him and flung him at me.

I got him by the ankle. He nearly tore me loose, but I had a handhold in a split rock and I hung on. He doubled on his own length and pulled himself down my forearm until he was flat to the ground again.

"Thank you," he bellowed.

"S'okay. I wish you could have seen your expression." I was rather pleased with myself, as if I'd managed to catch a glass somebody's elbow had knocked off a table. *Good reflexes, Carpentier!*

"We'll fly out of here," I screamed happily into his ear. "We'll fly over the wall. We'll build a glider!"

"I was stubborn too, once. Perhaps I still am. Is this really your wish, Allen?"

"Damn right. We'll build a glider. Listen, if we're light enough to be blown away by the first wind, we probably won't need much more than a big kite! Hey, let's get out of this wind and talk it over."

We crawled.

*   *   *

The weather changed as we lost altitude. It didn't get any better. The wind died down; we didn't need to clutch at the rocks, and we could hear ourselves speak. But a freezing drizzle started.

Now that I was thinking *glider,* the loss in altitude bothered me. "We need a place to build it," I said. "Out of the wind. We need fabric, a lot of fabric, and we need wood. We probably need tools."

Benito nodded. "There is a place, a great swamp, the Styx. Trees grow there. As for the fabric and the tools, we can cross the Styx and get them from the wall."

"How many walls have you *got* here?"

Benito smiled grimly. "None like this one ahead. Red-hot iron."

I believed him. Nothing subtle about Infernoland. "How far down is it? We're losing altitude with every step."

"A good distance yet." Benito laughed. "A glider. You may be the first ever to think of that. If we can launch from the hill above Styx, we can use the thermal updraft above the red-hot walls. Ecch," he said, about the time I stepped backward into freezing slush.

We'd reached another level region. I stood up and looked around. Freezing muck in all directions. Human beings lay full length in it, like half-immersed logs. The rain was turning to sleet. Cold garbage washed against my ankles.

"Behold the low-rent district," I said.

I got a chuckle from Benito. "Not yet," he said, and if I hadn't had the shivers before I got them then. He swept his arm about him and said, "The Gluttonous."

"I don't want to know. Come on, let's get through this."

We waded out into it.

In the darkness, and half-blinded by sleet, I managed not to step on any half-buried victims. Some raised their heads to watch us pass, showing us uniform looks of weary despair, then sank back after we were gone.

Men and women in about equal numbers, they ranged from pleasantly plump to chubby to gross. Three or four were as bad as the woman in the Vestibule. I wondered if they'd be pleased to know about her.

And once I wiped frozen slush from my eyes, cursing imaginatively under my breath, and when I dropped my hand he was staring at me: a long-haired blond man built like an Olympic athlete.

"Allen Carpentier," he said sadly. "So they got you too."

I looked close and recognized him. "Petri? Jan Petri! What are you doing here? You're no glutton!"

"I'm the least gluttonous man who ever lived," he said bitterly. "While all of these creeps were swilling down anything that came near their mouths, from pig meat to garden snails—and you too, for that matter, Allen—I was taking care of myself. Natural foods. Organic vegetables. No meat. No chemicals. I didn't drink. I didn't smoke. I didn't—" He caught himself up. "I didn't hire you as my lawyer. Why am I bending your ear? You're here too. You were one of the PIGS, weren't you?"

"Yeah." He meant the Prestigious International Gourmand Society, whose purpose in life was to go out and eat together. I'd joined because I liked the company. "But I'm not staying. This isn't my slot."

He wiped slush from his face to see me better. "So where are you going?"

"Out of this place. Come along?" He'd be unpleasant company till we got him a bath, but I knew he wouldn't slow us down. There never was a health nut to match Petri. He used to run ten miles a day. I figured he'd be a lot of help building the glider.

"How do you get out of Hell?"

So they'd convinced him too. "We go downhill for a while. Then we'll—"

He was shaking his head. "Don't go down. I've heard about some of the places downhill. Red-hot coffins and devils and you name it."

"We're not going very far. We're going to build a glider and go over the walls."

"Yeah? And then where?" He seemed to think it was funny. "You'll just get yourself in more trouble, and for what? You're better off if you just take what they give you, no matter how unfair it is."

"Unfair?" Benito asked.

Petri's head snapped around. "Hell yes, unfair! I'm no glutton!"

Benito shook his head, very sadly. "Gluttony is too much attention to things of the earth, especially in the matter of diet. It is the obsession that matters, not the quantity."

Petri stared a moment. Wearily he said, "Bug off," and sank back into the freezing muck. As we left him I could hear him muttering to himself. "At least I'm not *fat* like those animals. I take *care* of myself."

I was annoyed with Benito. "You didn't have to insult him. We could use his muscles. *Hey*—"

Benito heard the panic in my voice. "Yes?"

"I was at Petri's funeral! All that attention to his

health, and then he got caught in the Watts riots. But they damn sure didn't freeze him! They cremated him!"

"Freeze him?"

I didn't bother to explain. They'd cremated Petri, burned him to ash and gasses. How could he have been revived? How could the Builders of this Infernoland even have found specs for a robot analogue? Or a cell for cloning? Or . . . anything? Cremated is as dead as you can get!

Do the Builders have a time camera? Physical principles unknown, but to re-create Petri they have to be able to photograph the past. So we give them that, and the space-warping fields, and the genetic engineering that created Minos and freed Carpentier from the need to eat or drink or sleep, and the weather control, and the reduced mass of people in the winds, and the engineering technology that built Infernoland itself.

Carpentier, if they're that powerful, do you really want to fight them?

Of course not. I only want out!

"You're very thoughtful," said Benito. "Watch your step."

I stopped at the brink of a precipice. Then I followed Benito down a wandering, dangerous trail. It switchbacked along the face of the cliff, and in many places it would have been easy to go over the edge. That scared me a lot. After all, I'd done it before . . .

At least we were going down on our feet, and the sleet had stopped.

Things were definitely looking up. Still, there were funny noises from the gloomy area below, sounds

my mind registered as construction work. *Crash*. A
long pause, in which voices screamed orders too dis-
tant to make out.

   Crash.

7

THE TRAIL LED OUT ONTO A FLAT PLAIN OF HARD baked clay. As we reached the bottom Benito stopped me silently, with an arm held straight out across my chest. I was willing. I had heard the rumble and the shouting coming toward us.

It rolled past us at a good clip: a boulder four or five yards across, nearly spherical, bounding across the cracked adobe, surrounded by a shouting mob. They were urging it along, running alongside and butting the mass with their heads and shoulders, a mob of men and women dressed in the finest rags I'd ever seen. There were the remains of evening gowns and slashed velvet Restoration clothing, academic robes and Gernreich original creations, all torn and filthy.

The leader wore striped trousers and swallowtail coat and a ring that would have choked a hippopotamus. "This time!" he screamed at the top of his voice. "This time we'll . . . get them!"

"We can pass now," Benito said calmly.

"What was *that* all about?"

CRACK!

I looked to my left. Two nearly identical masses of pale-blue translucent stone stood rocking back and forth. Eighty or ninety humans in decaying opulence lay about the rocks as if they'd been flung in handfuls.

A few started to get up. The leader shook his fist and screamed, "Hoarders! Misers! Next time— Come on, men, we need a bigger lead time!" More got up, shaking their heads dazedly, and two groups attacked the two huge stones and began painfully rolling them in opposite directions. The other outfit, the one furthest away, was dressed differently: also in rags, but these had never been much to start with.

"Hoarders and Wasters," said Benito. "Natural enemies. They will try to crush each other with those rocks for all eternity."

"Benito, I'd swear those rocks . . ."

"Yes?"

"Skip it. I'm getting so I'll believe anything." We started across the plain. A couple of hundred yards ahead of us was a hedgerow of some kind, and sounds filtered through it. The misers were rolling their rock back that way, getting good distance for another run. We followed until they reached the hedges and stopped. Then they turned to, pushing it the other way. A prim-looking bearded man in the remains of a dark suit from the 1890's shouted toward the other mob. "You threw away the good in your lives! Now pay!"

I couldn't stand it any longer. I grabbed a wild-eyed matron by the shoulder. She struggled to get away. "Let me go! We have to crush those wasteful—"

"Ever manage to do it?"

"No."

"Think you will this time?"

"We might!"

"Yeah, sure," I said. "What would happen if you stopped rolling the rock and took a break?"

She studied my face for signs of idiocy. "They'd cream us."

"Suppose you both stopped?"

She pulled away from me and ran to put her shoulder to the boulder. The mob heaved it over a bump. She shouted back to me. "We couldn't trust *them*. Even if we could . . . we can't stop. Minos might . . ."

"Might take it away," I guessed. "I *thought* I knew that color."

Several of them glanced at me suspiciously. A couple of the men left the rock to advance on me.

"Hey! Hold on! I couldn't steal it by myself. I don't *want* to."

They relaxed. One, a man wearing the remains of a peasant smock, said, "Many of us hae been here for unco time. Yon Queen Artemesia says when first she came, there were still facets upon't. It must hae been a bonny sight." He sighed wistfully.

It must hae been, yeah. *Hey, Carpentier, how long would it take to wear all the corners off a twelve-foot diamond?* I turned back toward Benito. He was talking to someone on the ground.

It was a man with both legs crushed. The rock must have rolled over him. He was still in shock, because he wasn't screaming in pain, but he would be. Blood seeped from the jellied mess that had been his legs.

"For pity's sake," he said, "pull me out of the way. Maybe they won't get me a few times, and then I'll be able to keep away from them—"

He'd had it. Mind gone with his body. It was just

as well. We ought to be taking him to a hospital, but why bother? He'd had it.

"We are leaving Hell," Benito said. "First we go down—"

"Oh no! I know what they do to you down there! Just move me, just a little, please?"

I wondered where to put him. The ledge was hard and flat, baked adobe, with no cover between the cliff and the hedgerow. But we couldn't leave him out here. I took him under the arms and dragged him over against the cliff to die in peace.

"I thank you," he whispered. "What's your name?"

"Allen Carpentier."

He seemed to brighten. "I had all your books."

"Hey! Did you?" Suddenly I liked this man.

"Too bad I don't have my collection. I could get your autograph on them. I had . . . all of everyone's books. Did you ever hear of my collection? Allister Toomey?"

"Sure." I'd known many book collectors, and they'd all heard of Allister Toomey, to their rage and sorrow. Toomey had spent a considerable inheritance on books, all kinds of books, from double four-edges to first editions to pulps and comic books that were just getting to be worth owning. Much of what he had owned had been unique, irreplaceable. He'd kept them all in a huge barn he'd managed to hang onto somehow.

He'd spent everything else on books: there was no money left to take care of them. They moldered in that barn. Rats and insects got into them, rain dripped through the roof. If he'd sold a few of them he'd have been able to take care of the rest. I'd known a lot of collectors, and they all had a tendency to brood over Allister Toomey.

"I guess I don't have to ask why you're here."

"No. I was both a . . . hoarder and a waster. I lay between both groups . . . I suppose it's fair enough. I wish I'd taken . . . one or another of those offers. But what could I sell?"

I nodded and turned away. He continued talking, to himself now. "Not the complete Analog collection. Not the Alice in Wonderland. It was autographed. Autographed!"

Good-bye, Allister Toomey, who'd died twice now. I waited with Benito until the mob swarmed past with their bouncing boulder, then we ran across.

CRACK!

We found a hole in the hedgerow and scrambled through.

There was only a narrow ledge beyond the hedgerow, then a cliff. Thick mists hid the bottom, but it was a long way down. There didn't look to be any way over it.

We walked along for miles. There were other groups behind the hedgerow (CRACK!) all shouting and screaming (CRACK!) in various languages.

Then the sounds changed. Machinery, rivet guns, hammers ringing, the sounds of workmen and their tools.

Tools! We'd need tools for the glider. I began to run ahead.

A tremendous chunk of the ledge had collapsed, and the chasm ran right across, from the cliff on the downhill side to the base of the cliff towering above. A stream ran through it, and it had cut the gorge even deeper. Far below we could see people working frantically on a dam.

Another group was just as frantically tearing it down.

At our own level there was a similar contest. One

group was trying to build a bridge across the gorge, and another worked to disassemble it. Fifty yards in either direction were more bridge builders and destroyers. It seemed like a lot of wasted effort.

I looked to Benito, but he only shrugged. "I have never been to this part before. I do not think Dante came here either."

The group just in front of us were steelworkers, slapping together I beams, girders, plates, anything they could manage, fastening it with hot rivets and hammers. A small forge blazed away to heat rivets. I looked at all the work without comprehension— until I saw Barbara Hannover.

Suddenly it came to me. I'd known Barbara a long time. She wasn't cruel, and she didn't hate people, but she loved wildlife more. Whatever anyone proposed, a new bridge, a new freeway, housing development, mine, power plant, oil well, or wheatfield, she had a million reasons why you couldn't do it. I honestly think she'd have let all the Kansas wheatfields go back to prairie and buffalo if she could have thought of a way to manage it.

Add to her fanatic streak a Harvard Law School degree and one of the sharpest brains in the country, and it was easy to see why lovers of progress shuddered when she took an interest in what they were doing.

And naturally she was tearing the bridge down. I had an idea and looked closer at the construction workers. If Barbara was in this part of Infernoland, Pete couldn't be far away . . .

And there he was, bucking rivets. Pete and Barbara had been married for a while. A short while. Just as she couldn't see a housing tract without wanting eviction writs and bulldozers, he couldn't see a nice place on the trail without wanting to improve it with a log cabin. I'd gone hiking with him once.

The whole fifty miles was one long development plan, with ideas for improving the trail, building hostels, constructing artificial beaver dams, putting in hand-rails where the climb was steep . . . I almost killed him before we got back to the car.

"It makes sense," I told Benito. "Artistically. The way anything else down here makes sense. Pete and Barbara were both fanatics."

Neither of them had noticed me. I couldn't see how steelworking tools would help anyway. But up-stream was a wooden trestle bridge, with a group just finishing it while another tried to get at it with saws.

I looked at the saws and lusted. With a saw and nothing else we could build a glider. Other things would be useful, but they were easier to make than a saw would be. I had to have one.

The funny thing was that they used each other's tools. One guy would be hammering away to put a beam in place, and another would be sawing it in half—and while they screamed insults at each other, they did nothing else. The rules in Infernoland were more complicated than I'd have thought.

Or the robots were programmed funny.

But that sure looked like Pete and Barbara.

I waited until a progressive type laid down his saw, then started for it. Too late. A thin-faced woman grabbed it and had at the trestle-piece he'd been trimming to fit.

The next time I was quicker. When she set the saw aside for an ax, I grabbed it. There was a drill bit on the ground next to it, just a twisted chunk of steel more valuable than its equivalent in diamonds, and I got that too.

You'd have thought they *were* diamonds. Madam Hawkface started for me with the ax, and her builder companion was right behind. He didn't need an ax. He could have made three of me.

"Run!" I shouted.

Benito heard. We dashed for the trail leading down into the gorge. It was narrow and twisted, but it looked safer than what we were leaving.

I'd done one thing. I'd got those two crews to cooperate for the first time since Infernoland was opened to the public.

Unfortunately, what they wanted to cooperate on was tearing me to pieces. The trail turned a corner, then swooped down the cliff. We followed it.

8

THERE WAS A LEDGE TEN FEET BELOW THE LIP OF the cliff, and we stopped for a moment to catch our breaths. I thought I felt the cliff tremble and asked Benito about it.

"It is not any place to stay," he warned. "Allen, you will find that there is no safe place in Hell. Where-ever you stop—well, you won't like it."

"I can believe that." The thing to do was get out of here, and the more I thought about it, the better the glider looked. Now I had a saw that I could use to cut frames and ribs and stringers, if I could find anything to cut.

I still wondered what we'd use for fabric, but somewhere there had to be a storehouse for the costumes. The gowns Benito and I wore would do. It was a close-woven fabric, very tough, and it shed most of the dirt and muck we'd crawled through. I lifted the hem and tested the weave by blowing through it. It didn't let much through. It would do fine.

The ledge heaved again. I wondered if this were something for our benefit, then laughed at myself.

Earthquakes on call? The Builders were powerful, but *that* powerful?

We scrambled along the ledge until we were stopped by a waterfall pouring out in front of us. The water was black and dirty, and it stank like a sewer outfall, but the water rushed downward, and it had carved a bed in the cliffside. There were handholds in the sides of the notch the stream had carved.

How long would it take a stream to carve that? It would depend on what the rock was made of. And of course the Builders could have carved the notch themselves, though it looked natural enough.

After a while we reached the bottom of the cliff. The ground fell away at a steep angle. We found a path down it, along the stinking stream, twisting and turning along lower and lower, with steep cliff edges in places.

It would be an ideal place to launch a glider if we could get one up the slope. Drag it up here and over to one of the drop-offs, and push. Yeah. It looked better all the time, but first we had to build the glider, and what was I going to build it out of? I wanted to see those trees. I clutched the saw closer to me.

Benito was staring at me. I stared back.

"Forgive me," he said. "You hold that tool in a way I have seen before."

"Yeah?"

"By monks riddled with self-doubt, and clutching a crucifix to reassure themselves their religion is true."

"We'll *need* this. We'll need other things too. Wood, and rope for the glider—"

"Will that do?" He pointed downward.

We were almost at the bottom now. We faced a stinking swamp. Thick fog hid most of it, with only temporary glimpses through. Things thrashed around in the filthy water, but there were also bushes and trees hung with vines. Wood! Vines! Certainly I could build a glider out of those! "Now all we need is fabric. There must be a supply dump in this place. Or a laundry. Something."

Benito sighed. "There is."

"Great! Can we get a lot of those gowns?"

"It will not be easy."

"Easy?" I laughed. "Who cares, as long as we get *out* of here!"

Benito's determined look was very like a bulldog's. "Very well. I will help you get what you need. I will help you build your glider. I will help you fly it, in whatever direction you choose. In return, you will promise me that if this mad scheme fails, you will come with me to the real exit."

"Yeah, sure, sure." I wasn't really listening. I was too interested in the swamp below us.

The things bubbling around in there were people. Some of them just lay there half submerged, bubbling out filth and talking nonsense. Others fought each other, for what I couldn't make out. They roiled the stinking waters, washing up slimy things. Thick fog hung all around, and I had only glimpses of anything more than a few feet away.

"This way." Benito waded out into the slop. He seemed to know what he was doing, because it wasn't very deep, just to our ankles. The goop squished inside my sandals, slimy and thoroughly unpleasant. Every now and again there was solid ground a few inches above the muck.

We picked our way through low-hanging trees and bushes. I fingered the wood and tried my saw on one of the trees to cut off a branch. It seemed strong enough and quite springy. I hacked off a chunk of vine, and it was too tough to break.

We could! We really could build a glider!

As we got deeper into the swamp there were fewer people, but I could hear curses in every language I'd ever imagined, people screaming at each other, and the sounds of blows. Sometimes a filthy shape would try to climb up onto the ground where we walked, but others would grab it and pull it back into the mire. I shuddered. Why did they do that?

"The wrathful," Benito said. "And the sullen. The worst offenders in upper Hell." He was about to say something else, but he ran into something lying on the trail and almost fell.

It was a man, filthy with the muck, lying in fetal position. His eyes were open and staring at us. He glared, not at us, but at the universe in general.

"Hello," I said.

"Come with us," Benito added. "There is a way." He didn't sound hopeful, and of course there wasn't any response. "Remember there is a way. Downward, accepting everything—"

"Come on, he's catatonic." It bothered me, Benito preaching to a rubber-doll catatonic. Was my loony-bin theory right after all? Psychodrama on the grand scale?

Then why was I here? And Jan Petri, and Pete and Barbara? It was as if the Builders had revived everyone who had ever lived! Then set out to cure the crazy ones. Did they think I was one of those?

There was another one on the trail, and he wasn't catatonic at all. He stood there glaring at us, while others thrashed in the muck at either side of him. To get past we'd have to wade out into that, and from the ripples we would not only be over our heads but among the fighters. They'd never let us out.

"Excuse us," Benito said pleasantly. "The trail is wide enough for us to pass if you will step forward two paces."

"Bugger off."

"Surely you will not stand in our way?" Benito was still very pleasant, but there was an edge to his voice.

"Took me a hundred years to get up here," the figure said. "*You* never *have* been in the muck. If it's good enough for me, it's good enough for you."

He was a big man with powerful arms, and he seemed to mean it.

"Stand aside," Benito said. He was giving orders now. "You may come with us if you will—and if you can, which I doubt. But you will not prevent us from going." Benito's voice still had the ring of authority that had cowed Minos, and it shook the guy momentarily.

"Don't I know you?" he said. He stared at Benito. "I'm sure I know you. Well, whoever the hell you are, get past me the same way I got up here."

"Friend, you leave us no choice," Benito said.

"Aha! I *do* know you! You're Ben— Hey! Let go! Hey!"

Benito grasped him by the shoulders and lifted him as easily as I would a child. I gaped as Benito flung him out into the marsh. He wasn't even breathing hard. "Come, Allen."

"Yeah. Sure." I followed numbly, wondering who Benito really was. A professional wrestler? Circus strong man? What he'd done wasn't impossible. I'd seen it done before, but not often, and Benito didn't look that strong.

9

EVENTUALLY WE GOT THROUGH THE TREES AND BRUSH to open water. There was a big black tower at the edge. I couldn't see anyone in the tower, but suddenly there was a light in the top window. It flashed, ruby-red, out across the marsh.

Red? Ruby? A laser! Not magic, just a laser signal from an old stone tower. Far out in the murk over the water there was a flash of light, blinking, the same color as the signal.

"Phlegyas will come for us now," Benito said. "You must be careful. Say nothing you don't have to say, and as little of that as possible. Let me handle him."

"Sure. Why?"

"Because we are fugitives and we are approaching the, ah, administrative centers of Hell. There are demons here. Guards. They can do terrible things to us."

"Can't they just." I'd seen enough atrocities already. Were the Builders the crazy ones? They seemed to like pain.

From somewhere behind us there were screams of

rage and agony, and splashing noises. I thought I saw ripples in the open water ahead of us too.

Then something took shape in the gloom ahead, something moving toward us.

It was a boat. A big man, bearded, with a low gold crown on his head, stood in the stern with an oar in a sternlock. He sculled slowly, but that boat *moved*. I almost laughed. He certainly wasn't putting out enough effort to get that kind of speed. The boat must have a hidden water jet or something.

"I have you again!" the man crackled. "Ah, Benito, caught again. Good work!" He looked at me closely, and his grin faded. "Who are you?"

I didn't answer.

"Were you sentenced to lower Hell?"

"Phlegyas, mind your own business," Benito said. "Bring the boat to the shore. I do not care to wade in your filthy swamp."

"Don't like cold, eh?" Phlegyas seemed to find that funny. "Well, you won't have cold feet long, where you're going! Get in, Benito, get in. The other one has to stay here, of course. I have orders concerning you, but not him." He looked at me again. "You don't have a pass from Minos? No papers? You can't come."

"He will come," Benito said. "This has been willed where what is willed must be. Now bring the boat to shore."

Phlegyas shrugged. "All right, all right, you have the formula." His voice was a nasty whine of complaint. "It's sure been hell here since Dante published that book. You'd be surprised how many try that on me. Nothing I can do about it, either."

We scrambled onto the boat and sat gingerly. I noticed that the boat didn't sink deeper by an inch. Didn't we weigh anything? In that case we could walk on the swamp! But that was silly, because the swamp rippled and bubbled with people—and we'd sunk to the ankles in the muck. I could smell the stink on my feet.

Every now and then a nose would appear above the water as someone caught a breath, then vanished again. How many were there in that swamp? I could hear screams of rage and agony and pain, and cursing in all languages, but I couldn't see any details in the half-light and the fog.

Phlegyas sculled rapidly, and the boat shot away from the bank. The fog enclosed us in a circle of dark water rippled with shouting faces and with the chicken guts and other filth that poured down from the land of the Hoarders and the Wasters.

Sometimes a filthy claw would reach from the water to clutch at the gunwhales, and then Phlegyas would smash it with a six-foot pole he kept in a socket ready to hand. He sculled easily with one hand.

"You know, that formula doesn't work with the real supervisors," he said. He reached to straighten his crown and gave us a sour look. "They took the power of decision away from me. I made a couple of mistakes, just a couple of lousy mistakes, and now they think they can do better than me. Over two thousand years of service here, and upstarts have more power than me. It isn't fair, you know. Bastards. Stupid bastards. But they won't let you in without a pass, you watch and see."

"Old man, be silent," Benito said.

"Humph." Phlegyas sculled more rapidly. The boat shot through the water. Now I could make out dim glowing red. The fog began to lift, and we could feel the heat.

There were walls ahead of us. They had towers, and some of them were cherry red. The radiated heat was already uncomfortable. A low, wide mudbank stretched out from the walls to the swamp, and I could see a landing dead ahead, at the end of a narrow bay.

We headed toward it. A man came out through a doorway in the wall. He was old and bent, and he hobbled. He carried a box about a yard square and an inch deep.

He shuffled to the water's edge and used a shovel to fill his box with mud. Then he turned and ran, his robe flying out behind him as he darted back into the door he'd come so slowly out of. It didn't make sense.

I turned to Benito, but he only shrugged. He didn't know either.

We passed the entrance to the bay. "You may let us out at this landing," Benito said.

"Nope." Phlegyas continued to scull.

"It would be more convenient."

"Yep."

"Then why don't you do it?" I demanded.

"Because I don't have to," Phlegyas answered. He continued to scull until we reached another landing. "Regulations say ferry terminal to ferry terminal, and that's where I go. Nothing about stops in Himuralibima's Bay."

Benito frowned, but we didn't say anything. The boat reached the dock area. There was no one to meet us, and I wasn't sorry.

"Off, off," Phlegyas shouted. "There's more coming. No rest for an old man, none at all. Off, off." He reached for his cudgel, and we scrambled ashore before he could smash us with it. As soon as we were off he was sculling away, headed for the other shore like a motorboat.

The city was maybe a quarter-mile away across hard stinking mud. The walls were hot, although not as hot here as further away. A mile to our left was a tower that glowed cherry red.

Thermals! There'd be thermals here, if a glider could get across the swamp. It would take luck, and we'd have to drag it pretty high up that cliff to make it, but it could be done.

"Be very careful," Benito said. "I will have to deceive the officials. Do not undeceive them."

"You mean you're gonna lie? Oh, Benito, that's sinful. You could go to Hell for telling lies."

He took it seriously. "I know. It is one reason I am here."

"Um, but this *is* in a good cause . . ."

"I thought my deceits were in a good cause." He shrugged. "The Commandment is against false witness, and by extension against malicious deceit, and fraud, and perversions of honesty and honor. We shall not do that, and as you say, it is in a good cause. Or so I hope. We tread dangerous ground, Allen."

"Come on," I said. I started off toward the door I could see ahead of us. Fat chance I'd ever make that joke with *him* again.

It was getting warmer all the time. Off to our left, near the blazing-hot tower, were the remains of a *big* gate, torn off its hinges. Things walked guard duty in front of it. They were just far enough away, and there was just enough fog and steam, that I couldn't see them clearly. But the shapes seemed odd, twisted out of true. I didn't want to ask about them.

We came to a Dutch-type door open at the top and with a counter on the lower half. Heat poured out through the opening. A bored-looking man in a high stiff collar, something out of a Dickens novel, was inside in a little office. His face was narrow and pinched, and the heat couldn't have improved his disposition. He had a desk like a woodcut from the Scrooge story, a tall thing he stood at. There wasn't a chair or a stool in the room. We waited at the counter.

And waited, and waited, getting warmer and warmer, while the clerk fussed with papers on his desk. He seemed to be reading every line on an enormous form a dozen pages thick. Every now and then he used a red pencil to mark something. When he continued to turn the pages and scrawl notes without even looking at us, I pounded on the counter.

"Are we invisible?" I demanded.

"A moment, sir. Just a moment, please. We're very shorthanded here, sir. You'll have to wait, sir." He made each "sir" a curse.

"You would be well advised to attend us." Benito's voice had that edge to it, a note of warning. The clerk looked around uneasily. He obviously didn't recognize either of us. Hardly surprising.

"Your papers, please."

"We have none," Benito answered.

"Oh my, oh my, one of those days," the clerk muttered. "Well, if you haven't any papers, you can't come in. The rules are very strict. You'll have to go back for papers." He turned back to his desk and started looking over the files on it.

"We have an errand inside," Benito said. "You do not help your record by delaying us."

The clerk looked back nervously. He examined us closely again, noting the slime on our gowns and the stench of our sandals. That seemed to cheer him. "What is your station inside?" he asked.

"No fixed post," Benito answered.

"I can't help you, sir. I'm only record-keeper for the Sixth Circle. Next window, please." He turned back to his desk. We waited. Benito whistled something monotonous. Finally the clerk turned back. "You still here, sir? I *told* you, next window, please."

"It is to the Sixth Circle that we must go now."

"Why didn't you *tell* me," the clerk complained.

"Very well." He reached into a cabinet and produced what looked like manuscript books and short stubs of pencil. "If you don't have the proper papers, you'll have to fill out these forms."

They were twenty pages long, covered with small blanks, and there were nine copies. Not only wasn't there any carbon paper, but the blanks were arranged differently on each copy, although they all asked for the same information.

"I think we will not bother," Benito said.

I flared up. "What the hell do you want all this for? Great-grandmother's blood type! Why should I fill this out?"

"You *have* to." The clerk was getting more and more irritated. "You can see they're all blank. You can see they have to be filled out. Right at the top, see, it says, 'Replacement for lost papers, application for, D-345t-839y-4583, to be submitted in nine copies.' I can't do anything for you without that information."

"Aren't there exceptions?"

"Of *course* there are exceptions, *sir*. One was made over two thousand years ago. Before my time, but they still talk about it." He shuddered. "But you are obviously not Him. Is either of you a living man? Can either of you summon angels? Those are in the book too." He glanced at a shelf of loose-leaf folios above his desk. "Volume sixty-one, page eight ninety-four, paragraph seventy-seven point eighty-two—I'm *glad* we changed to the decimal system, but most of us didn't like it—it says very plainly, anyone who can summon angels may pass. But if you're applying under that ruling you'll have to go to the main gate. *Don't* prove you can do it. Just go to the main gate, and they'll take care of you."

"But you will not let us pass," Benito said. "Not

even if I tell you that if you do not you will be in grave trouble?"

"I know my duty. You will not come through."

"Very good. You have done well," Benito said. "If you had let us in, we would have reported it. Now you have a favorable report coming. Who is your supervisor?"

The clerk stared at Benito. "Mrs. Playfair. Formerly a postmistress. But—"

"Oh, my," said Benito. "I won't be able to help you after all. It would do no good to give the report to *her*."

The clerk was unsettled. "Why not, sir?" The "sir" wasn't a curse any longer.

"I am not permitted to say."

"Ah. You mean—" He gulped. Whatever he imagined was going to happen to Mrs. Playfair worried him excessively. "But what will happen to her people? What will become of *me*?"

Benito looked crestfallen. "You know the rules—"

"But I've done everything *properly!* My files are in perfect order—oh dear, oh dear, I *told* her she shouldn't have let that man in the records room, I *told* her he wasn't properly credentialed, I *told* her! It was all her fault, I *told* her . . . my files are in perfect order. And they won't even look at them, they'll just—" He was actually wringing his hands as he looked around his office at his desk and files.

Benito frowned. "It would be a waste to have you in the boiling pitch—"

"IN THE PITCH!" the clerk screamed.

"Are you certain your files are in perfect order?" Benito demanded.

"Of *course* they are! Here, you can see for yourself." He did something that opened the gate.

Benito and I crowded in. Benito took down a vol-

ume of the rule book and leafed through it. "Keep
this up to date, do you? All revisions in place as they
come in? Where are your unfiled revision sheets?"

"There are none," the clerk said primly.

"Hmm." Benito lifted the forms on the clerk's desk.
"This is not in order!" He leafed through quickly.

"But I hadn't checked the seventh copy yet!" the
clerk moaned. "I was doing that when you interrupted
me! You can't report me for that, I was trying to give
you service, and—"

Benito handed the forms back. The clerk looked
through and extracted a bulky set. There was pencil all
over the first six pages, then the writing medium
changed to something darker. Benito looked at it curiously. "This is hardly legible."

"He used up his pencil," the clerk said. "Volume
four, page ninety-eight, paragraph six, states that no
applicant can have more than one pencil. So I made
him fill it out with something else. He used blood."

"His own?" I asked.

"Where else would he get blood?" The clerk turned
to Benito. "Who *is* this man?"

"In my custody. Witness. Not your case, don't worry
about it." He handed back the forms. "This seems to
be in order."

"Thank you." There was relief all over the clerk's
face.

"One item was very difficult to read. You should
be more careful next time."

"Yes, sir. Certainly, sir. Are you finished with it?"

Benito nodded. The clerk took the form—copy
seven of nine copies—and tossed it into a wastebasket
in the corner. It burst into flames. I stared. A man had
used his own *blood* to fill that out? I glanced at the
forms the clerk had handed us.

Sure enough, at the top of copy seven, it said "DE-

STROY." Copy eight went to "APPLICANT" and copy nine was "TO BE ROUTED TO THE STATISTICAL SECTION."

"What will be the charges against Mrs. Playfair?" the clerk asked, his voice low and confidential.

Benito frowned. "I understand there are shortages in uniforms and supply—"

"But we don't have anything to do with that."

"Precisely," Benito said knowingly. Comprehension dawned on the clerk's face. He nodded.

"We're going to check that now," Benito said. "Keep up the good work, uh—"

"MacMurdo. Vincent MacMurdo. You'll remember?"

"Certainly." Benito opened the inner door and held it for me. I went through, trying not to hurry.

10

BENITO FOLLOWED AND CLOSED THE DOOR BEHIND him. I slumped against the wall, convulsed by silent laughter.

I jumped away fast. The wall was burning hot. I smelled scorched cloth. Another second and I'd have had a bad burn.

We were in a corridor that stretched to infinity in both directions. It was about ten feet high and wide, and there were doors at intervals along it. People hurried in both directions, paying us no attention.

And there were all *kinds* of people! Men and women in flowing robes, in US Post Office uniforms, in colonial costumes, in the high collars the Dickensian clerk had worn, military uniforms, Chinese mandarin robes, modern business suits, coveralls with insignia of planets and stars and sunbursts, a whirl of scurrying humanity shoving past us as if we weren't there.

Nobody was going to notice us for our funny clothing.

The old man we'd seen outside rushed past us, almost running. He carried a box of fresh mud and poked at it with a stick as he ran. We watched as he turned through a door and out of sight.

Someone had stopped beside us and was laughing. He wore a Roman toga.

"Do you speak English?" I asked.

"Certainly." He was still laughing.

"Who *was* that?" I asked.

The laughter stopped, and the man glared. He was carrying some kind of wood plank with wax on it. There were letters cut in the wax. "You are new here?" he demanded.

"From another division," Benito said quickly. He lowered his voice. "Special assignment."

The Roman drew away from us. "Surely you have no interest in Himuralibima? He is our most honored civil servant."

Benito gave a knowing look. I still had a blank stare.

"Hammurabi's secretary, you know. Invented record-keeping."

"Ah," I said. *Hammurabi? Oh, all right, he's Hammurabi's secretary. And I am Napoleon Bonaparte.* "You'd think after all these years they'd let him slow down a little."

"But he *can't*," the Roman protested. "They've offered him retirement, but he has to fill out the proper forms, and in his case, of course they're in cuneiform. And you have noticed how hot it is in here?"

I couldn't stand it. I tipped my head back and roared with laughter. It rolled out, gales of laughter, choking me, as I thought of that first bureaucrat trying to complete his retirement papers before the mud dried from the heat . . .

. . . Himuralibima's *Bay?*

Benito merely nodded. "Fitting. I am certain you have work, Signor—?"

"Uh, of course," the Roman said. "Your pardon." He pushed past us and walked briskly down the corridor. Our clerk came out of his office. The Roman stopped, and they talked in whispers.

"Allen, must you ask unnecessary questions?" Benito demanded.

"I'm a writer. Of *course* I ask questions."

"Please do not. Not in here. For the moment we are safe. They think—" He motioned with his eyes.

I turned my eyes only. The Roman had stopped someone else and was whispering to him. The man he'd stopped, a young man in 1930's US Army uniform, nodded. Pretty soon he stopped someone and both looked clandestinely at us. They stopped others . . .

"They're telling stories about us," I said.

"Yes. Let us hope they are telling the proper ones. Now we must find the supply center."

Wherever we went we were preceded and followed by whispers. People got out of our way, too. If we wanted to go through a door, if we even looked like we wanted to go through a door, there was a scramble to hold it open for us.

"They sure are scared of you," I said. "They know who you are." Which was more than I did.

"I think few of them have seen or heard of me," Benito answered.

Oh, really? "You know your way around here."

"No. I know my way around bureaucracies. This one is no different from any other."

"You were a bureaucrat once?"

He hesitated. "I suppose you might say so."

"Exactly what—"

An anguished voice drowned me out. We were passing an open door, and a woman's voice screamed in rage and pain: "But that form is twenty-seven pages long! All that for one tool?"

I looked in, caught a familiar hawklike profile, turned back and kept walking. "Don't look now," I said out of the corner of my mouth.

The other voice followed us. "You should keep better track of your handsaw. The rules are very clear . . ."

At the next door there was a long line of naked people, fat men, pretty girls, ugly women, studs, every form and variety of mankind: the reception desk at a streakers' convention. They were trying to get to a counter where some fat guy handed them clothing while two beanpole women took information down on more forms.

What was this? The supply center for Infernoland? Were these employees, or spectators, or—

—or what?

We got in line, the only ones with clothing who did. A thin guy in a medieval bachelor gown came in, went behind the counter, and whispered to the supply clerk. The clerk summoned his two old biddies, and they whispered together.

Finally one of the women came out from behind the counter. She wore a coverall of a kind I didn't recognize, dark blue with strange insignia. "What may we do for you?" she asked. She was trying to be pleasant, and it was obvious that she'd never learned how.

"This man was given the wrong clothing," Benito said. "He is wearing the same thing I am. In our section we do not give a junior courier the uniform of a supervisor."

She frowned. Benito didn't look like he was dressed as a supervisor. He looked like an escapee from the violent ward. So did I. But he only stared back, and after a while her eyes dropped. "What should he wear?" she said.

"Loincloth. And there are nine senior men in my section who have loincloths and no gowns. It is intolerable."

"Oh." She didn't know what to make of that. She went back and whispered to the other biddy.

Meanwhile the line moved up. The clerk looked at papers and then at the fat man at the head of the line. He went into the shelving stacks behind the counter and came back with bright gaudy clothes, slashed velvet sleeves and tight trousers. They were obviously too small.

"Ungood. Double plus ungood. Too small. Wrong period," the fat man protested.

"Tough shit, buddy. We all got our troubles. Next!"

The biddies came over to him and whispered. He looked at us. "Uh, you sirs—can I help you?"

Three helped carry the gowns, and a fourth brought up the rear with stacks of papers flowing with seals and ribbons. Benito paid no attention to me; he just walked ahead as if he assumed we'd all follow, which we did.

We turned a corner, and he stopped. "This will do," he said. "Give those things to Allen. You have your work to do, and this is his task."

"Certainly, sir. Is there nothing else we can do for you?" This one wore a policewoman's uniform, vaguely American, though the shield was shaped strangely. She talked without using articles. When she spoke to her subordinates she used a language I didn't know. I was afraid to ask her death date.

"I said this will do," Benito said. "We will be met by others. You may go."

"Thank you, sir." The sow turned and stalked away, followed by the others.

When she was out of sight Benito seemed to wilt. His straight posture was gone, the high angle of the chin vanished, and he slumped.

Then he laughed. "So. Nothing changes. Now we must get out of here before someone tells this story to an internal security agent."

"They think—what do they think? That we're important officials?"

"No. Of course not. They know we are only pretending that."

"Then what—"

"But they cannot be sure. We *might* be important officials. But most of them think we are secret police."

"But how do you know there *are* secret police?"

Benito looked very sad. "Allen, there have to be. You cannot run a bureaucratic state without them. Come."

We found a door to the outside, and Benito surrendered one of the documents he'd collected. We passed through and were out on the mud flats again. A stinking breeze wrapped itself around me, deliciously cool, and I said, "Ahh . . ."

Far to our right the old man had just filled his box of mud again. He ran for the gate, writing frantically.

11

I WAS SMILING AS I TURNED. THE ROBES I HELD stacked on my head, an ungainly load. "Now what?"

Benito was staring across the swamp. "I don't know."

"Ah?"

"We cannot possibly persuade Phlegyas to take us back. I fear we must swim." He set his own stack of robes down, shook out the top robe and used it to tie the rest together.

Swim? Through *that?* It wasn't the garbage that turned me off. It was the bubbling of angry people in and under the water. If we met anyone like the guy Benito had thrown back into the water . . . if we met half a dozen of them while loaded down with heavy wet stacks of robes! "Wait a minute, Benito. Let's try something else."

"Lead on, then, Allen."

I stopped to tie my bundle as Benito had tied his.

Then I turned right along Himuralibima's Bay. The choice was deliberate: here there were windows and doors along the wall.

I was wading thigh-deep and not liking it, but it was the only way to learn what I wanted to know. At worst I was postponing our swim. At best—"We've got plenty of time. You keep saying so."

"So we do. I wonder what you expect to find."

My foot brushed something soft.

She was clearly visible beneath two feet of water: a long-boned black woman with her hair floating like seaweed around a slack face. I asked a stupid question. "Is she dead?"

"Of course," said Benito.

She was curled in fetal position. She stayed rigid as I rolled her to bring her head above water. There was no sign of decay, and no sign of life. But I felt for a pulse in her neck and found it.

"Catatonic." And I started to get mad. "Another catatonic. Of all the dirty things. *We* don't persecute crazy people for crimes. What right do the Builders have to put crazy people in Hell?"

"The Builders?"

"Never mind. Of all the dirty things. Benito, can you handle two bundles for a minute?"

He took my robes on his other shoulder. He waited while I reached into the water to adjust the woman's position.

Catatonia. It's a rare enough disorder, but almost incurable. You can find one or two catatonics in almost any mental hospital. They afford opportunity for endless jokes, all identical, for a catatonic will take any position you put him into and hold the pose indefinitely.

Every intern thinks he is the first to see the possibilities. He will lead the resident catatonic to the hospital cafeteria, place him just outside the door, and leave him there with his thumb to his nose or his middle finger rigidly extended. Hilarious!

Sometimes he gets a surprise . . .

I had to stand on her knees to straighten her legs, but finally I got them stretched out in front of her. She was still leaning too far back, her eyes staring at infinity through a half-inch of scummy water. Still standing on her knees for leverage, I reached beneath the water, took her shoulders and pulled her up to sitting position.

Now she'd be able to breathe.

. . . sometimes he gets a surprise, your antic intern. He will have just finished adjusting the patient's hand with thumb properly to nose, when the hand becomes a fist and the fist becomes a missile warhead. Catatonics are hideously strong. They have to be, to hold one position forever.

And she was sitting down. She lashed straight out and tried to punch a hole through my groin. She damned near made it. I whooped and doubled over, sucking air. Sucking, as it turned out, filthy water as I rolled helplessly over into the swamp.

I tried to uncurl. My lungs still wanted to suck water. Inch by inch, I fought my mouth to the surface, drew a lungful of sweet stinking air, and screamed.

Benito was sloshing toward me. I gestured him back. If he dropped the robes to help me, they'd quadruple in weight!

He stopped. I waited for the pain to ease a little, then tried to stand up. When I put weight on my legs it felt like she'd hit me again. I moved toward shore, doubled over.

The woman's lower lip was just at the surface of the water. She held her arm straight out, fist clenched. "Don't make waves," I told her sourly as I passed. She didn't respond, and she still looked dead. Water streamed from her nose.

I didn't stop for any more catatonics. Gradually I was able to straighten up. Benito followed patiently, carrying both bundles, both of us wading thigh-deep in water. I ignored the floating garbage. It wasn't getting me any dirtier than I already was.

The texture of the bottom had changed. Beneath a film of frictionless mud there were tilted slabs that had sharp corners and tended to slide . . . I stopped. Benito stopped behind me.

I said, "Feel that?"

Benito didn't get it. "What should I feel?"

"Himuralibima's Ford, that's what! No telling how far it goes, but it should get us a good distance across the swamp. Here, give me that." I took one of the bundles and started into the swamp. The footing was chancy, the slabs tended to slide, but it was better than swimming.

And I, feeling that I had earned the right to brag, bragged. "All along I wondered where the dried mud was going. It'd shrink a little when the water evaporated, but even so, that bay is *huge*. Where do they dump the slabs after Himuralibima gives up? Maybe I'd find a mountain of them. Or maybe they don't want a pile of ruined clay slabs in their working area. Maybe they're afraid of getting ticked off for sloppiness.

"So, I was right. Someone's been dumping the slabs in the bay. Every hundred years he has to walk a little further. Otherwise they'd show above the surface."

"Very clever, Allen."

"Thank kew." No telling how far it would go, but we were a good distance into the swamp, and the water was only up to our calves. *Hold your breath and make a wish, Carpenter. Or just hold your breath, the water could be over your head any second.*

We were nearly across before it ended. The slabs dipped, and I followed the dip, walking on eggs, with the stack of robes balanced on my head. I was chin deep where the mud turned squishy soft.

So far, so good. I found an underwater ridge and followed that, going waist deep, then higher. I was wading ashore, with Benito behind me, when our luck ran out.

The broad-shouldered man who blocked our path was the same who had blocked our path before. He shied back when he recognized us, and then he saw our situation and grinned.

I turned back to Benito. "Mind if I try this?"

"If you think it will help."

"I wrote science fiction, remember? I ought to be able to explain a complicated idea to a moron."

I hadn't lowered my voice. The broad-shouldered man advanced on us, saying, "Who's a moron?"

"Don't worry about it," I told him. "You've got worse problems than that. Remember the flying lesson?"

His grin was back. "I'd like to see old Benito try that with his arms full of bedsheets!"

"He won't be able to," I said, keeping my speech slow and distinct. "He'll have to put them down. In the swamp." Pause. "They'll get all dirty." Pause. "Imagine what that will do to his temper."

I watched his eyes. It was getting through to him.

I said, "Why don't you step aside while you think it over?"

"Some guys would rather talk than fight," he said contemptuously. He turned and stalked back to his point of high ground.

PART II

12

"THINGS ARE DEFINITELY LOOKING UP FOR ALLEN Carpentier."

"I beg your pardon?" Benito was looking out at the marsh, at decaying trees embedded in fog.

"We've got a quiet place to work, I've made some flint tools, and there's everything we need for the glider. What more could we want?"

Benito sighed, and I got back to work. The first job was to find a place to loft the glider. We were on a little area of high ground, no more than thirty yards square and nestled up against the base of the cliff. The bad-tempered character was between us and everyone else. He wouldn't let anyone else past, and he wasn't about to bother us. I could just see his back through the mist.

First things first. I used a log to flatten out an area larger than the glider would be, then cut a long springy sapling for a ruler. After a while I had a whole collection of saplings of various lengths and thicknesses.

You draw the rough outlines, then spring the batten

—in this case one of the saplings—across the important points. That makes a smooth fair curve. It was the way the Wright Brothers designed airplanes, and it was the way the Douglas Gooney Bird was designed. It wasn't until World War II, long after the age of flight was underway, that airplanes were designed on drafting tables. Before that they were done on the loft floors, the same way that boats were designed for centuries.

I don't know how long it took me to get it right. I wasn't in any hurry, and Benito never tried to rush me. After a while he even developed some enthusiasm.

Did you ever try to set up ribs and make them keep their shape by tying them with vines? When the ribs are whatever you can cut off swamp willows? As a lesson in patience the job has few equals . . .

Eventually it looked liked a glider. The wings weren't precisely symmetrical, and the control surfaces pivoted on wooden bearings with dowels shaped by flint knives and thrust into holes enlarged by flint drill bits; the fabric was sewn with vine tendrils shoved through holes poked with a thorn; but it *looked* like a glider.

I remembered the Cargo Cults of the South Seas.

The islanders had been sorry to see the airplanes go after World War II ended. Native magicians had made mockups of airplanes and landing fields. It was sympathetic magic intended to bring back the real airplanes and the great days of cargo and trade. I told Benito about the Cargo Cults, amusing him greatly, and only later realized what had brought them to mind.

What I was building would never look like more than a crude imitation of an airplane. But it would fly!

I spent as much time making tools as I did working on the sailplane. A bow drill: take one bow, as for

shooting arrows; get a good curve in it, and instead
of an arrow, take a piece of sapling. Wrap the bow-
string around the piece of sapling. Attach the drill
bit to one end. You need a hard block in which the
top of the sapling chunk will rotate freely because
you've worn a depression in it. Hold that block in
one hand, put the drill point where you want it, and
draw the bow back and forth with the other hand. The
sapling turns. The point turns. In about a week you
can drill a hole.

I'd heard that boatbuilders in Asia preferred their
bow drills to American electrics. They must have
been crazy.

I worked. There were no distractions. The Builders
must have altered my body radically. I didn't get
hungry, thirsty, horny, or sleepy, and I never had
to go to the bathroom. I wondered what I had become.
What was my power source now? A power source
with no food intake and no waste outlet? If it was
beamed power, Benito and I would be turning ourselves off when we dropped the glider beyond the wall.

Beyond the wall . . . I hadn't thought much about
that. What would we find outside? Dante had described a dark wood, a wilderness. Why not? A low-
gravity world, native vegetation allowed to run wild . . .

No guarantees, Carpentier. There might be nothing
but Infernoland itself, a tremendous cone built in air-
less space, with a point mass, a quantum black hole
for instance, mounted at the tip to provide gravity.
In that case we were dead.

I kept working.

And eventually, there it was. The Fudgesickle, by
Carpentier and Company. "This is a demo, madam.
The finished model will have many other desirable
features, such as landing gear and seats for the crew,
and metal fastenings . . ."

"Will that hold together?" Benito didn't seem particularly worried. His tone was more one of abstract curiosity.

"I think so. We shouldn't put much strain on it, but I've noticed we don't weigh what we should. Infernoland seems to be built on a lower gravity planet than Earth."

"Yours is the most curious delusion I have yet encountered here. Well, if it will fly, we may as well try it. The sooner you are done with this idiocy, the sooner we can reach the center and escape."

I could have killed him. So the Fudgesickle wasn't a thing of beauty. It would fly! And it was a lot better way out than his.

I didn't try to kill him for three reasons. First, he'd break my neck. Second, he *had* been useful as a guide; he'd gotten me the fabric. Third, I needed his help getting the Fudgesickle high enough on that cliff above us for a launching.

We pulled the glider up the slope and carried it until the land fell away as a steep cliff. The swamp bubbled like sludge, with sickly lights glowing among the odd-shaped bushes and trees.

"If we crash down there, we'll never get out," I said. "Can you fly this thing?"

"I have flown them." Benito laughed, with real humor.

"What?"

"I have done this before. We launched the glider from a much higher cliff. An Austrian soldier came to get me out of a sticky situation." He settled himself at the controls.

Something familiar about that story . . . but Benito was looking out at the swamp, and I didn't ask him. He looked awfully big and heavy to be a glider pilot, and I had to remember that we didn't weigh what we should. I strained against the fuselage and shoved outward.

It wouldn't have worked if we hadn't been massless or nearly so. Even then I kept wondering about that. It chewed at my soul the way a ragged tooth attracts the tongue. How could we have weight and no mass? The wrong weight, and . . .

Infernoland. Disneyland of the Damnable. How long had they kept me in that bottle? Clarke's Law kept running through my head, an old axiom of science fiction: "Any sufficiently advanced technology is indistinguishable from magic."

In my time it would take magic, the supernatural, to make that many people, not weightless, but *massless*. It wasn't even possible in theory to extract the inertia and leave the weight. But *they* could do it, the Builders, the God Corporation. Why? It must have cost a lot. Just how big a paying audience did they have?

Who was watching us now?

I heaved against the plane, and then there was no room for thought. The plane dropped like a rock, with me hanging onto the tail, crawling forward to get into the rear seat. Benito knew how to fly, all right. He let us dive, just missing the cliff, until we had built up speed; then he leveled out, taking us above the swamp and toward the red-hot city.

Dis. Dante had described it, glowing with red-hot mosques, with demons on the walls to guard it. I didn't see any demons. I'd take them on faith. If the Builders could build Minos, they could make demons.

We were about a hundred feet above the swamp, and keeping steady altitude. There must have been warm air rising from the hellish brew below us. Then we were over the wall, and Benito banked sharply left to catch the updraft. The plane rose steadily, gliding along the gentle curve of the wall.

Benito shouted, "This won't do any good, you know."

"We're getting higher, aren't we?" I pointed down. The swamp had shrunk until I could see the gentle curve of the cliff beyond it. Cliff and red-hot wall were concentric arcs of circles.

The view to the right went down forever. Beyond what seemed the biggest maze ever built, steam rose in a thick curtain. Through wind-torn rents in the steam I could glimpse factories belching out ugly black dirt, a line of electric pylon towers, a yellow glow of desert . . . on and on, down and down.

What had it all *cost?* Thousands of times as much as Disneyland. What kind of people would build Infernoland and people it with unwilling damned souls?

If this worked out, I would never know.

We were higher than the cliffs to our left. It seemed that we had climbed fast, faster than we had any right to. But we were nearly weightless and completely massless. The plane had only its own structural weight to lift. We continued to rise until we were in the hideous gray fog that served Infernoland for a sky.

It stank: excrement, oil, smog, sickness, slaughter-houses, everything hideous. There wasn't even the honest smell of sweat and locker rooms.

"We'll have to turn now," Benito said. "We can't stay in the updraft if we can't find it."

"That's right. Go!"

We banked left, then straightened out. The fog began to thin. We were doing it! Passing over the rings we'd struggled through. A wind full of weight-less people bounced us about, then let us go. We passed over Minos' palace. It was even bigger than

I'd thought. There was the wall ahead. We were going to make it.

Have at you, Builders! You can't keep a science-fiction writer in Hell!

Even so, no hero worth writing about would have left Infernoland with so many questions unanswered. He would have led a revolution against the Builders, and never mind the odds. The plane would have been for reconnaissance, not escape.

Heinlein, van Vogt, "Doc" Smith, Robert Howard, all the men who wrote of mighty heroes: what would they think of me now? *Who cares? Go, Carpentier! Go, go!*

The villas of the First Circle slid below us.

And suddenly we were losing altitude again. The plane dipped sharply just over the cold river. I should have known it would.

"We're not high enough!" I shouted.

"Obviously. What now?"

"Take us back to the thermals! Get up higher, we can try it again."

"As you wish." He didn't say it wouldn't work. He just banked left again and headed us back down into the bowl. Toward the winds.

Even below the gray fog, Infernoland's lighting was not good. Gloom and night, all the way down. Infernoland was a vast funnel, leading down, down . . . down where Benito said we had to go. And we were flying there.

Suddenly we were in the winds. People flew about us like flurries of autumn leaves, some together, some alone. Aerial whirlpool ahead, which Benito avoided. And off to the left a straight updraft, flailing human shapes rising helplessly toward Infernoland's invisible roof. Just before they vanished into the gray stinking fog, the air column topped out and they streamed away to both sides.

"There," I said. I pointed.

Benito shrugged expressively.

"I'm getting pretty damned tired of your defeatist attitude!"

He banked toward the updraft. Suddenly we were rising as in an elevator. I caught startled faces, and some of the whirling victims tried to swim toward us through the air, but they were rising faster than we were. They couldn't catch us. I was glad. Massless they might be, but if I could feel wind roaring past my ears and tugging at my hair, then people clinging to the wings would foul the airstream. We'd all crash.

We left the updraft and were carried along with the others. Sure enough we were just at the edge of the fog, so that we could hardly see below. This was it! We were as high as we'd been above Dis, and much closer to the wall. "Now!" I shouted.

Benito even grinned at me as he turned toward the wall. This time we'd make it!

As he banked, something bulky hit him in the face and knocked him back into the seat, then slipped past and wrapped itself around me. I struggled to rip it off, and it fought back. We'd picked up a passenger.

"Let me at the controls! I used to be a glider pilot!" The hitchhiker pulled himself off me and scrambled into the other seat.

Benito didn't resist. "Let him fly," he said.

The plane turned sickeningly. We had lost altitude. I could see over the stranger's shoulder: cliffside, swampland, a glowing red line—

A tailspin, and we were beyond the place of the winds, headed back into the inner circles of Inferno-land.

He pulled us out of the spin. Nothing subtle about

it. He just stopped the spin with the ailerons, then pulled back on the tailflaps and hung on. Presently we were flying level again, headed toward the swamp. The stranger looked back at us, showing a lean, cheerful face beneath short, wind-tossed hair. "Where to?"

"Up and out. Over the wall."

"Good thinking, but there's a problem." He waved toward the cliff. We were well below the level of the winds.

I said, "There are red-hot walls down there. Good thermals. We'll spiral around them until we're high enough, then get back into the winds—"

"Not me."

"We have to! There are updrafts in the winds. Before you interfered we were high enough to get out of this place."

"Down is correct," Benito said.

"Not the way you mean!"

He shrugged. "It is the only way we can go now."

"No question about that." We headed out over the swamp again, feeling the rising air that was just strong enough to keep us level. If we didn't find an updraft we'd crash in the swamp.

The trouble was, we were looking for something invisible. You can't see a wind, you can only see what it does. I was looking for heat turbulence, or formations that might break a horizontal airstream and send it upwards; *anything*. There'd been no problem spotting updrafts when the wind was full of actors or draftees or whatever they were.

Ahead through the murk we could see the cherry-red glow of the walls of Dis. It looked a bit like the first sight of a town in the middle of the Nevada desert, and for a moment I thought of food and coffee and one-armed bandits, and girls . . .

We were over a hot-spot in the swamp. A shape

rose from the murk and shook a fist at us. He had a big bushy Afro hairdo. He lost interest when another man in a voluminous white gown and high pointed cap rose up to scream at *him*. They were locked in battle when we left them.

"Take it easy," I told our pilot. "I think I saw the left wing bend way up when you pulled us out of the spin."

"Yeah, I saw it too. What did you build this thing out of?"

I told him. He looked uneasy. I asked, "What kind of gliders are you used to?"

"Hypersonic."

"Eh?" said Benito.

"Huh?" I said.

The stranger chortled. "Jerome Leigh Corbett, at your service. I was a space-shuttle pilot. I had a dozen flights on my record, and then . . . You ever have one of those days?"

"Damned right," I said. Benito laughed and nodded.

We seemed to have enough altitude to reach the hot walls. They were close enough that we could make out details through the murk and the red glow. Corbett seemed to know what he was doing.

There were ripples in the dark mud below. A hand thrust itself upward, middle finger extended. There was no movement in the cobwebs and slimy moss hanging from the bushes, no wind, nothing; only the ripples in the mud.

"One of those days," Corbett said. "First, a twenty-six-hour hold while we replaced one of the solid boosters. That was only irritating. We lost one of the three main motors going up. Then after we made orbit one of the fuel tank clamps jammed. Either of you know what a space shuttle looks like?"

I said I did. Benito said he didn't.

"Well, the tank is big and bulky and cheap. We carry the main motors down aboard the dart, the winged section, but we leave the tank to burn up in the atmosphere. If we couldn't get the tank loose there wouldn't have been any point in going down."

"Did you?"

"Sure. We fired the orbital motors in bursts until the clamp sprang open and let us loose. Then we had to use more fuel to get back to our orbit. We were supposed to dump cargo and change orbit, but there wasn't enough fuel. We had to go down."

Benito was looking totally confused. It must have been gibberish to him. I asked, "What happened?"

"I don't know. I spacewalked out and looked at the fuel tank clamp. I swear there was nothing wrong. But maybe the metal fatigued, or maybe the hatch over the clamp lock got twisted—anyway, we were halfway down and going like a meteor when we got a burnthrough under the nose. I heard the maintenance techs—they were the cargo I couldn't jettison —screaming in the instrument room, then the whole nose peeled back in front of me. I woke up by that ferryboat. The crowd pushed me along to Minos, and he threw me into the whirlwind."

"And why were you there?" Benito asked.

Corbett grinned. "Being a shuttle pilot carries a lot of prestige. The girls liked me."

We were over the walls of Dis now, and banked to catch the rising air. My seat surged comfortingly against me . . . and the left wing bent in the middle. The Fudgesicle turned on its side and dropped.

Corbett dropped the nose. The wing, relieved of pressure, straightened out. But when he tried to pull up it bent again. We'd have been better off if the loose section had ripped away, but it hung on, dragging us back.

Corbett did his best. He tried to fly with the broken wing, the flap raised high on the right wing to compensate. We got some lift that way, but there wasn't any doubt: we were going to crash.

Inside the walls of Dis there were tombs. Dozens, hundreds, thousands of tombs, some glowing red hot, others dark. The whole landscape was littered with them.

On the walls themselves were—beings. They didn't look much like the cute little devils in Disney cartoons. They raged at us, and Corbett, seeing them, dove for speed to get out of their sight.

The wing folded entirely. Corbett played the controls like a virtuoso at an organ, heading out over the tombs and toward a steamy clear area beyond and below them, but we were too low and falling lower, into the tombs—

We dropped into their midst. The plane kissed the top of one tomb, bounced, and smashed nose on against a wall of red-hot iron.

13

FLAME ROARED UP AROUND ME, AS IF A FUEL TANK
had caught. I pulled myself loose and rolled out,
clawing frantically with my hands as the flames
washed over me. When I tried to get to my hands
and knees my right leg wouldn't work. I pulled myself along the ground, dragging the useless leg behind
me, whimpering with fear while the fire raged behind
and the air I breathed grew unbearably hot.

I didn't stop until I was forty feet away. My fingernails were torn, and my hands cut on the flinty ground.
I rolled over onto my back to look behind me, afraid
to look at my leg, knowing I'd have to. What had I
done to myself?

Someone was screaming.

I ignored the deep throbbing incoherent pain in
my leg to look back at the crashed glider. Benito had
been thrown clear in the crash. Now he was running
back toward the glider.

Corbett was trapped in the wreckage, rammed up
against the red-hot iron tomb, screaming like a damned
soul. I didn't even consider trying to get him out. He'd

be dead in seconds. His skin would already have charred away, and he was breathing superheated air and smoke. How could he scream like that with seared lungs? He was a dead man.

Benito hadn't thought of that. He ran straight back into the flames. I watched in disbelief as he pulled at Corbett's arm, getting nowhere, while fire roared about him. Benito took flaming wreckage in his hands and heaved it away, clawing to get Corbett out.

Idiot! He'd leave me stranded here, my leg ruined, with no guide and no one to help me! I sat up and tried to go to his aid, but agony flashed in my leg. I had to look down.

I stared at two splintered ends of red-and-white bone protruding through my thigh. Bright blood spurted through the torn skin. Arterial bright, impossibly red. I couldn't take my eyes away.

Once before I'd broken a bone. I'd caught a football wrong in high school, and a knuckle cracked. It had made me sick, not just the pain, but the thought of that broken thing inside me. I could hardly walk to the clinic. Now I stared at two ends of a broken thighbone while my life's blood jetted out with each pulse. I expected to faint. But nothing happened, and presently I thought of making a tourniquet before all my blood was gone.

There was only my robe. I gripped the hem in my teeth and pulled with both hands. It wouldn't tear, and wouldn't tear, and bright blood jetted in the air.

Benito! I was lying with a broken bone and a terrible wound, but I could be saved! Why was Benito wasting his time on a hopeless case, a man he'd barely met, a *hitchhiker?* It wasn't fair.

Corbett was still screaming as Benito tore at the wreckage. Where did the pilot find the strength? He should be finished, lungs burned out, heart stopped, but he went on screaming mechanically as if the sounds of pain were being ripped out of him.

The pilot came lose suddenly, and they both went sprawling backward. Benito got up and dragged the pilot over to me. Benito was parboiled and hairless, his hands blistered and burned. Corbett was a charred corpse, black from end to end, with blood-rare steak showing through cracks in the char. There were no eyes left in the sockets. And still sounds came through the swollen blackened lips. I wanted to stop my ears.

"Stupid!" I said. "Stupid, stupid, stupid! In a minute he'll be dead anyway!"

"He will heal," said Benito. "He is dead already."

"*Heal?*"

"Certainly."

Agony surged in my leg. I looked down . . . and couldn't look away. I watched in helpless fascination.

The blood had stopped pumping. The bone ends gradually vanished as skin crawled out to cover them. It crawled on, closing the wound, leaving my leg in an odd tented shape. Without my willing it the leg straightened slowly.

An old scar I'd once got fishing slowly reappeared where before there had been bloody jagged bone end. The pain turned to a ferocious itch. That went away too.

I was healed.

Corbett had stopped screaming. Now he only moaned softly. I looked, afraid to look, afraid not to. The char was flaking off him in thick patches. The skin beneath was bright sunburn red, not at all like raw meat. His tattoo, like my scar, came up from underneath his skin like a self-developing photograph. He groaned again and opened his eyes.

There were eyes in the sockets. Corbett looked at me

and smiled weakly. "Can't die again, I guess. Wished I could for a time there."

"It is a pointless and evil wish," said Benito. "The dead cannot die."

"No." Corbett began an inspection of his body.

I stood up uncertainly. Benito watched, saying nothing. I was able to stand. I could walk. I did. I went off a way, toward the glowing tomb, until the heat was nearly unbearable, and I stared at it.

We'll have to change our theory, won't we, Carpentier? Corbett's no robot. The Builders would have had to put new, sunburned skin under the skin to be charred. They would have had to plan all this ahead of time. They would have to be omniscient.

And what about your leg, Carpentier? *What about your leg?*

Biological engineering. Rapid regeneration. That, to add to their other powers. They can warp space and possibly time. They can take the mass from a human body and leave the weight. They can put Minos' tail into—where? Hyperspace? They've got fine-tuned weather control and infinitely adaptable robots.

And they can engineer your body, Carpentier, *your* body, in such a way that it heals in minutes, and do it without your knowing they gave you that ability.

Getting a little thin, isn't it, Carpentier? A neat set of rationalizations, but it won't work. How are these Builders different from God Himself? What can God do that they can't?

And back at the edge of my mind I couldn't help remembering the last thing I'd screamed in the bottle.

Corbett had got up and was peeling saucer-sized flakes of charred skin from his chest and shoulders. "Hot here," he said.

I nodded and abandoned my reverie. It was hot. Even the tombs that weren't glowing were just below red heat. Here and there flames shot up from open pits. It must have been painful for Corbett with his new skin.

I remembered where we were. Inside the walls of Dis. How were we to get out again? We were surrounded by hot glowing tombs, flames, fire, heat everywhere, except in one direction where darkness showed through the red glow.

"We have to get out of here," I said to Benito. "We'll roast to— We'll roast." To death? We couldn't die. Can't die twice, Carpentier.

"Of course we must leave," Benito said. "Recall your promise. I helped you with the glider, and it did not work. Now you have no choice. We go downward."

"Which way?" For that moment I didn't care.

"I am not sure. We may as well go where it is more comfortable." He led us off toward the dark. It drew us onward, promising relief from the heat and the choking air. We threaded our way between heated tombs and great vatlike pits with fire dancing from them. Huge lids that would just cover them lay beside each one.

The edge of the hot region was the beginning of a white marble maze. The heat stopped as if we'd gone through an insulated doorway, but there was no door. I wasn't even surprised. It would take more than invisible heat barriers to surprise me now.

Corbett staggered into a corridor and sank down with a happy sigh, his back against cool marble. He wriggled to get his head clear of the brass fixtures.

We were in an endlessly sprawling building. The corridors were about fifteen feet wide and nearly that high. Every wall was covered with square-cut marble slabs and rows of brass plates and slender brass . . . what? Vases? I read some of the plates. *Name, birth-*

date, date of death. Sometimes an insipid poem.
These were burial vaults, and those brass things were
vases, and of course there were no flowers in them.
The corridor stretched on endlessly, and there seemed
to be branches at frequent intervals. Millions of
tombs . . .

"More unbelievers," I said.

"Yes," Benito answered.

"But I was an unbeliever. An agnostic."

"Of course."

"Why of course?"

"I found you in the Vestibule," said Benito. "But
now you know the truth."

A two-syllable response stuck in my throat. The
truth was an elusive thing, here in Infernoland. I
could talk about advanced technologies until Hell
froze over, and Benito would still call them miracles.

I'd watched a miracle. A compound fracture had
healed before my eyes. And I was no robot!

But this place had to be artificial. It was a con-
struct, a design. I *knew* that.

All right, Carpentier. An artifact implies an artificer.
There has to be a designer. Pick a Chief Engineer for
the Builders, and call him . . . what? Good fannish
names, like Ghod, Ghu, Roscoe, the Ceiling? No. Call
him Big Juju.

Question, Carpentier. In what way do Big Juju's
abilities differ from God Almighty's?

Size? This place is the size of a small planet. Carpentier, you've no way of knowing Big Juju can't build
even bigger. Worlds, stars, whole universes.

Natural laws? He suspends them at will. A world-
sized funnel, as stable as a sphere would be in normal
space. And—and he can raise the dead. Me! Corbett,
who couldn't *possibly* have been frozen. Jan Petri
the health-food addict, *cremated,* Carpentier, burned

to a pile of greasy ashes and a few chunks of bone, and now risen so that he can be tortured.

Big Juju can create. He can destroy. He can raise the dead and heal the sick. Was more ever claimed for Christ?

I looked back at the red-hot tombs. They still glowed with heat, but none of that reached us in these cool marble halls. "There are people in those tombs?"

Benito nodded. "Heretics."

The word was frightening. Heretics. They believed in the wrong gods, or worshiped the right god in the wrong way. For that they were raised from the dead so they could be tortured in hotboxes.

Iago says it. *"Credo in un Dio crudel."* I believe in a cruel God. And that you must believe, Carpentier. The ability to make a universe does not presuppose moral superiority. We have seen no strong evidence that Big Juju's moral judgments are better than our own. Would God torture people?

I half-remembered Sunday school lessons. No. But also, yes. It was one reason I was an agnostic. How could I worship a God who kept a private dungeon called Hell? That might be all right for Dante Alighieri, a Renaissance Italian! But Carpentier has higher standards than that!

A voice floated from within my mind, a tired voice whispering out of a mound of fat. *We're in the hands of infinite power and infinite sadism.*

We were in the private museum park of Big Juju. "We've got to get out of here."

"Too right," said Corbett. He paused. "Music?"

I listened. There was music playing from somewhere within these marble corridors. Something chintzy-sweet, a minor work by a major composer, played for every melodramatic sweet note in it. Artificial good cheer in Hell. "It fits," I said. "Granted we're damned, how do we get out? Which way?"

Benito looked around him. "I have never been in this part before."

"Not back out there," Corbett insisted. "Not unless we have to."

"Right. We've got time," I said. And I started laughing.

It was an awful sound. It bounced around in the maze and came back at me from all directions, transmuted to racking sobs. I tried to stop. Corbett and Benito were staring. I tried to tell them:

"I was right. Just once, I was right. All that time in the bottle, all that guessing, and I was right just once. Immortality! When they woke me up they had immortality." Dammit, I *was* crying.

Corbett took my arm. "Come on, Allen."

We went inward.

14

THE CORRIDORS BRANCHED AWAY, ENDLESS CROSS-
corridors in an endless corridor, and every one of them
the same, wall after wall of marble-sealed caskets,
each with its empty bronze vases for flowers. Our footsteps echoed hollowly. Our sandals hadn't been touched
by the flames. The sprightly music continued, never
getting louder, and the light never changed, neither
gloomy nor bright. On and on, corridor after corridor. Finally we halted.

"We haven't turned," I said.

Corbett nodded. "Do a one-eighty and we can get
out of here. Let's."

Half-facetiously I rapped on a bronze nameplate
and read off the name and dates. A translucent human
shape formed before me. I stared in horror, then
shrugged. What was a ghost among ghosts?

"Pardon me," I said. "Can you direct us toward the
wall of Dis?"

The ghost's voice was faint and reedy. "Wall? Dis?"
Faint laughter. "They must have added more exten-

sions to the Mausoleum. I don't remember anything like that in Forest Lawn."

"Very funny. This isn't Forest Lawn."

The ghost seemed vexed. "I was supposed to be buried in Forest Lawn. I paid for it before I died. It was in my will. Where am I?"

"Would you believe Hell?"

More faint laughter, as if from a great distance. "Certainly not. I don't even believe in ghosts." And then there was nothing but the wall.

I jumped when Corbett spoke behind me. "It's a risk, but are you game to try a cross-corridor? I think if we turn left and keep going straight we'll be headed up again."

The scenery changed. Now there were niches with urns in them, much closer together. We came to a T intersection and turned and returned to the right direction when we could. Then another T and a Y and a big round empty space with corridors off in all directions and a big monument in the very center . . .

. . . and we were in the good section of town. The sarcophagi were no longer buried in the walls. At the ends of short alcoves were huge marble oblongs, ornately carved, guarded by traditional statuary. Knights and vague sexless winged beings that were supposed to be angels and might have been faggots; reproductions of famous religious statuary; original creations, all done with enormous competence, all in monstrous bad taste. Sculpted Bibles open to John 3:16. Replicas of European cathedrals, done in perfect scale, bronze toys.

One alcove was blocked off by a brass gate and enormous lock. All the nameplates were of the same family, all ornately carved with relief pictures and bronze replicas of their life's signatures. We looked in, grinned at each other, and went on.

Pride. Unbelievably ornate monuments purchased at unbelievable price: expensive tombs turned prisons. I wondered if they matched monuments left behind on Earth. Sure, I decided. Big Juju has a sense of fitness.

Fitness?

In this one case, yes, fitness.

The corridors twisted again and again. The dead were high walls on all sides of us. Our footsteps were dull intrusions on music for the proud dead. The dead walked among the dead. Dead. Dead. *Dead. Dead!* Word and reality echoed with each step. Word and reality hammered at my soul. Dead. Dead. Dead. Presently I sat down against cool marble.

"Allen? What is the trouble?" Benito's anxious voice was far away.

"Come on, let's get moving. This place gives me the creeps." Corbett shoved at me with his toe. "C'mon."

I tried to speak. It wasn't worth the effort, but finally I heard my own voice saying, "We're dead. Dead. It's all over. We tried to make lives for ourselves, and we didn't make it, and we're dead. Oh, Corbett, I wish I'd died like you."

The gay sweet music mocked me. Dead. Dead. Dead.

Green light blinked on and off in the corner of my eye. It was annoying, a disturbance, an irritant in the thick cotton closing about me. I could see the source without turning my head, but it was an effort to move my eyes. Why bother? But the light winked on and off, and eventually I looked at the source, a neon sign blinking far down at the dead end of a corridor of the dead. It echoed my thought:

SO IT GOES
SO IT GOES
SO IT GOES

—off and on, endlessly, in green neon.

Unreachably far away, on another world, in another time, Allen Carpentier had been buried like a potato in a closed coffin ceremony. The fans had come to the funeral, some of them, and a few writers had come, and afterward they'd gone off to have a drink and talk about new writers. Carpentier was dead, and that was all there was to it. I could speculate forever about Big Juju's moral superiority, I could wander forever through Hell, and so what?

SO IT GOES
SO IT GOES

Corbett's voice came dimly. "We may have to leave him. I saw this happen to a guy, once, in the war. He's going autistic."

"I have seen it also. Many times. Would you leave him here?"

I thought Benito was shaking my shoulder.

SO IT GOES
SO IT GOES
SO IT GOES

—what was the blinking neon sign doing in this place?

A horrible suspicion filtered through the blankets around my brain. I pushed Benito away and surged to my feet. I walked, wobbling, toward the blinking light. So it goes?

At the end of the corridor was a tremendous square-cut edifice in black marble. The epitaph beneath the neon sign was long and wordy, couched in words of one syllable and short, simple sentences. A man's life history, a list of books and awards—

Corbett and Benito stared when I came back. Corbett said, "You look like you're ready to kill somebody."

I jerked my thumb behind me. At first I couldn't speak, I was that angry. *"Him.* Why him? A science-fiction writer who lied about being a science-fiction writer because he got more money that way. He wrote whole novels in baby talk, with sixth-grade drawings in them, and third-grade science, and he *knew* better. How does he rate a monument that size?"

Benito's smile was lopsided. "You envy him that tomb?"

"If you must know, I was writing better than he ever did before I left high school!"

"Being dead hasn't hurt your ego," said Corbett. "Good. We thought we'd lost you."

"He's got *vases* bigger than the bottle they put me in!"

"You were an agnostic. Selfish, but not viciously so," Benito said. "If I judge rightly from the size of his tomb, he must have founded his own religion. And possibly worshiped himself."

"No, they were jokes, sort of. But he did found at least two, not that there ever were any followers, or that he even intended there to be. One of them had everyone telling comforting lies to everyone else. The other was the Church of God the Fairly Competent. Maybe I should have gone in for something like that."

"Why didn't you?" Corbett asked.

"Because what's the point of mocking people who've found something to believe in." I turned toward the big, gaudy edifice. *"That's* the point."

Benito shook his head wonderingly. "I question your sanity. He is in there. You are out here, free to escape."

I didn't answer, but he was right. We turned away. For a time I could see the green reflection blinking ahead of us.

SO IT GOES

We were lost in endless corridors of the dead. Benito walked in stolid patience, but Corbett's face had acquired a grim, set look, desperation barely held in check. I kept my own thoughts to myself.

But I remembered Big Juju's ability to distort space and time.

We'd come a long way. Perhaps there *was* no way out.

And what if we did get out of the maze?

Benito said we had all eternity. Eternity in Infernoland. Or in Hell. Big Juju or God, it didn't matter; the problem was to escape.

I'd built a glider once, and it had flown. Get me through the wall, get me fabric for the wings, and I'd do it again.

But I'd have to do it without Benito.

You promised you'd go with him, Carpentier. Down to the center, out his way. You can keep your word or you can break it; but if you break it, it'll be without his help.

Suppose he's crazy? Or an agent for Big Juju?

Then you're on your own.

Nuts. Benito might be able to trick the damned bureaucrats into giving us whatever we wanted. I couldn't kid myself I'd be able to. Fabric I could get— at worst, by peeling it off catatonics—but how to get through the wall? I'd seen demons on the rim. More demons guarded the gate.

I glanced sideways at Benito. Stolid patience, and iron faith in God and the maps of Dante Alighieri. And Carpentier's given word. If we ever got out of this maze, he'd go down. We could follow or not.

I felt heat ahead. We turned a corner and found a wall of red-hot urns. The floor seemed to slant uphill.

Corbett whooped. "This way! To the wall!" His voice sounded out of place in the mausoleum. I waited for Benito to protest, but he said nothing, and I wondered if he knew something we didn't.

"We could make quite a safari," Corbett shouted. He was over-joyful at finding a way out. "Just open these urns and pour out the ashes."

"I went further than that, once," Benito told us. "I attempted to establish a local government."

"Didn't work?"

"No."

"Why?"

There was no answer. It became apparent that there wouldn't be one. Something else to think about.

We hit a T corridor and were back in cool marble. We followed it a short way, anxious lest we find ourselves back in the endless tombs. It turned left again. I rounded the turn ahead of the others and found myself facing red heat. I shaded my eyes—

"Your papers, please?"

I squinted through my fingers.

I faced a towering wall of red-hot iron, with a divided door in it. There was a counter on the lower closed half of the door, and someone behind it, half-hidden in the dark interior framed by bright red light. He held a stack of papers. The bored face showed no sign of recognition. It might have been the same clerk or a different one.

"Papers? Come on, I haven't got all eternity." He pushed the stack of papers toward me. "You'll have to make these out before you can go uphill. It's in the rules."

I backed around the corner. To the questioning looks of the others I said, "Don't ask. Just turn around."

We went back the way we'd come, looking for a right turn. Presently we found it, and—

"Your papers, please?"

I walked toward the booth, but I was studying the gate behind the clerk. Iron glowing red, but it was only waist high. We could jump it.

The counter turned white hot as I approached.

"Papers? You'll have to fill out the forms. No exceptions."

I looked to Benito. He shrugged and turned away. After a moment I followed, hating him. He wasn't going to help.

And he'd known it all along. We had to go downhill.

15

THE MUSIC WENT WITH US WHEREVER WE WENT: nature themes, melodramatic sweetness, singing violins, but never funeral dirges or somber tones. The cheerful music was more depressing than any funeral march.

Gradually I realized we could hear something else as well. I don't know if it had been with us the whole time, waiting for us to become aware of it, or if it began as we threaded our way deeper into Hell.

The sounds came from the tombs. Groaning. Whimpers. Croaks of rage. Mumbled curses. Once even gay whistling, a tune that jarred against the canned music.

Gradually the clammy air warmed. It was our first sign that we were moving out of the maze.

We followed currents of warming air. Where the air turned steamy hot we found a doorway.

Unnerving sounds reached us through the doorway: screams of agony torn from throats that could contain them no longer, blended with animal war cries and the most vicious curses I'd ever imagined.

Corbett plunged ahead, but Benito caught him. "Carefully," he warned us.

We looked out and down. The ground fell straight away from the doorsill, first vertically, then angling down to a forty-five-degree slope. The dirt was baked adobe with jagged edges of protruding flint.

The bottom of the cliff was obscured by steam, much like the marsh outside Dis, but this was hot. The steam roiled about, leaving occasional clear patches. Gradually the picture formed.

We were looking at an enormous discolored lake. The shore curved away to either side until steam hid the endpoints. Men and women stood waist deep in steamy red water, and they howled. They were packed like a public pool on a Kansas summer Saturday, and they wanted out.

Some tried it, but they didn't make it. Armed men patrolled the shore between us and the scarlet water. The guards were dressed for a costume ball, in the military garb of all places and all times, but they walked like sentries whose officers are watching. Their eyes were uniformly on the lake, and they held weapons ready.

Weapons: there was every hand weapon known to history. Pistols, bows, scythes, crossbows, throwing-sticks, slings, pikes and lances, AR-15 rifles, all held at the ready. When someone attempted to leave the lake, the sentries fired.

I saw a woman in black military uniform cut nearly in half by a burst from an automatic rifle. She shrieked in agony and waded deeper into the lake, where she stood, healing.

Healing. The implications of our inability to die began to get through to me then.

One man in a long beard wore a golden crown on his head and clustered crossbow bolts through his chest. He was stubborn. He'd move toward the shore. The crossbowmen would fire, and he'd stagger back, the scream hissing through clenched teeth. He'd pluck the bolts from his chest and throw them contemptuously into the water—and wade toward shore again.

And again. And again. He was a fool, but a brave one.

"I take it the guards won't be on our side," I whispered.

Benito shuddered. "No. On the contrary, if they catch us, we—" He didn't finish, but he didn't have to.

The guards looked silly in those costumes. I knew some of them. Nazi swastikas and American GI's. Coldstream Guards and Cameron Highlanders. Blue and gray of the Civil War. World War I helmets. Redcoats and the blue-and-buff of Washington's Continentals. Fuzzy-wuzzies and Chinese Gordon's Tommies, and more: Roman legion, Greek hoplite, vaguely Asiatic uniforms, long gowns and wicker shields, spears with golden apples on the hilts; and more still, yellow men in animal fur, red and black men in little besides war paint, blue men stark naked. Blue? Britons in their woad, marching beside legionnaires, followed by men and women in coveralls carrying tiny machine guns of a variety I'd never seen.

And they watched the lake, constantly, vigilantly. "They won't see us up here," I said. "Now what?"

"We must cross the lake," said Benito. "There is a place, far around, where it is only ankle deep. Elsewhere it rises to above our heads in the deepest parts. The damned stand at a depth appropriate to the violence they did on Earth."

"That water looks hot. It steams."

"It is boiling blood." Benito laughed without humor. "What would you expect for the violent?"

A frozen moment stretched endlessly. Then Corbett shouted, "We can't walk into that! No!"

"Jerry—"

"I've been burned before, remember? We'll never make it! When our ankles are cooked we'll go to our knees. When the legs are cooked we'll be lying in it!"

"Yet you see that every man and woman in the lake is standing."

The calm voice halted Corbett's panicky monologue. He looked. I'd already seen that Benito was right. If they could stand, their cooked legs must still be operating. They also wouldn't stop hurting . . .

"The guards will not allow us to wander freely in Hell," Benito cautioned us. "Without instructions regarding our sentence, they may well force us to the deepest spot and keep us there. You have noted that their weapons do not kill, but they can disable."

Let's stay here, Carpentier. I'm starting to like the music.

"They must not notice us. We must do as little screaming as possible." Benito spoke seriously, without a trace of humor. Benito had been in Hell so long that suffering was not remarkable to him, or even unusual.

"There may be a better way," Corbett said slowly. He pointed. "Allen, what do you see?"

"An island." Half-obscured by steam, it stood very low in the lake a good mile to our right. It was more crowded than the water around it, the water that Benito said was boiling blood.

Poetic justice. Infinitely exaggerated, as everything was here. No doubt the people boiling down there were murderers in life, or torturers, or kidnappers, arsonists perhaps. The violent. Well, at least we knew how to get across. "Benito, can we cross on the island?"

He stared pop-eyed, his big square jaw thrust forward. "I had no idea there was an island in Acheron. Dante did not describe it."

"I suppose he mentioned boiling blood?"

"Of course. He also described the ford I used before. The ford is heavily guarded, and perhaps the island would be better." He considered. "Dante did not mention the ship in Acheron either."

"Ship?"

"Yes, Allen, a wooden sailing ship sunken on the other side of Acheron. The decks are just awash with blood. I have been aboard it. There are grills in the deck and souls beneath the grills."

"Slave traders," Corbett speculated.

"Probably," said Benito.

But how had Benito been aboard? Was that where he had escaped from? Or from deeper down? I didn't dare ask, yet how could we trust him until we knew his crime?

How could we not?

"Slave traders aren't our problem," Corbett said. "I suppose the best plan would be to circle up here until we're just opposite the island, then make a run for it."

We looked at each other and nodded agreement.

We turned back inside to parallel the shore, passing walls of shelves packed with crematory urns. I savored the cool, damp air. I was going to miss it. The cliff edge was just beyond that wall.

Why bother, Carpentier? Why not stay here?

No. We've got to get out of here. Minos would track us down eventually, and then what? We have to escape.

Hey, Carpentier, what makes you think there's a way out?

I don't want to think about that. There has to be a way out. Benito says there is. Dante described it—

A way out for him, yes! A living man whose guide called on angels!

There is a way out of Hell and we're going to find it, because we can't die trying, because there's nothing else to do but sit for eternity. Eternity.

I'm scared, Carpentier.

Me too. Let's talk to the others. They're scared like you. Talking helps.

"The guards," I said. "They bother me two ways."

Corbett said, "It's *boiling* that bothers me."

"I don't think I'll like being shot full of arrows and bullets," I said. "But worse than that, what the blazes are they *doing* here?"

Corbett just laughed. They were guarding, his look said.

"They did violence they believed justified," said Benito. "They fought for what they thought was a higher cause."

"And there aren't any soldiers in Heaven?"

"I'm sure there are. But these enjoyed their work." His voice took on a note of sadness. "They enjoy it still. They do not seek to escape."

"It's weird. They're serving the Builders, or Big Juju, or God, whatever we call the master of this place. If they're serving God they ought to be in Heaven!"

Benito shrugged. "Or Purgatory. Perhaps. Theology is not my specialty. The next doorway is just ahead, be careful."

He wouldn't say more, but I remembered the uniformed servitors in Disneyland and wondered if the guards worked in shifts. Did they have homes to go to when they got off work? Did they go home and tell their wives about their day?

We waited, peeking around the doorjamb to watch the shore. The island was just opposite, no more than fifty yards offshore, obscured by clouds of steam and no easier to see than it had been from a mile away.

A band marched past, robed and unarmed. "Inquisition priests," Benito murmured. "They would call the temporal authorities. The soldiers."

They receded. A handful of barbarian women passed, arms and shoulders the color of their bronze armor. They carried bows and shortswords. Behind them was another group, also women, wearing olive-drab fatigues and carrying submachine guns. They passed out of sight, and the shore was clear.

"Run," Benito ordered.

We ran. There was a ten-foot drop to the steep slope. I landed on my feet and kept running in a half-controlled fall. Jagged flint edges tore at my feet. When I hit the beach I kept running, because I knew I'd never be able to *walk* into the boiling lake. The wandering clouds of steam wrapped me round, hid me from the guardians, and I ran toward the chorus of screams. The smell was overpowering, fresh blood and clotted blood, copper bright and polluted foul.

Corbett was ahead of me. He splashed into bubbling red fluid and screamed. He stood, covered to his knees, screaming in pain. Benito plunged in, waded through the stuff like a damned robot and gripped Corbett's arm to keep him from turning back. Then I was in it myself. I fell into a trench and was instantly waist deep.

The pain hit me weirdly, as if I'd stuck my finger in a light socket. Stunning. Unreal. All my senses were scrambled. I knew the smell of pain, its sight and sound, and there was nothing to see or hear but pain. I couldn't control my limbs. They thrashed and twitched, almost spilling me full length into the stuff.

Still jerking like a marionette, I turned toward shore. Nothing could be worth this much pain.

Half a squad of Green Berets stood there studying us. They had friends: small men in black pajamas.

I turned back. We were committed now. Through a gap in the steamy mist I had seen their eyes; dull, ex-

pressionless, intent on their task: and their task was to
let no one leave the blood.

"The island," I screamed. "To the island!" But I
didn't move and neither did the others. We stood where
we were and screamed.

"The island!" Corbett laughed hysterically, laughter
and pain and horror. "We can't use the island—"

I screamed, "What?"

"Stupid! Look!"

He was right. I cursed the rolling clouds that had
hidden it from view. They were shoulder to shoulder
over every square inch of the island. I never saw a
more vicious mob. They were armed haphazardly, with
clubs and crude daggers of what seemed to be splintered
bone. Even as I watched, someone trying to climb out
of the blood was repelled by half-a-dozen stab wounds.
He staggered away, howling, leaving a foaming red
wake.

Benito came up to me, still pulling Corbett by the
arm. "We must wade around the island."

I couldn't move. Suddenly he took my shoulder in
his powerful grip and began to plunge through the boiling red, towing both of us like children. I remembered
his strength. There was no point in struggling with him.
I didn't want to. I wanted *out,* but my limbs would not
obey. The pain was paralyzing.

You could read the agony on Benito's face. He hurt
as we did. But he plunged on. He shouted, "Deeper
down, there is a place where souls are not even allowed to cry! Here there is no law against screaming!"

"Yeah! Cheer me up!" I screamed.

We halted. There were guards on the shore. A man
in a high peaked hat stared through binoculars. We
didn't dare move.

There are two ways to treat constant excruciating
agony. Both involve screaming. You may try to sup-

press the screams, and they will force their way through your teeth; or you can just let it out. Similarly, you can concentrate on the source of pain and try to minimize it: a current of not-quite-boiling blood here on the left, get into it! Stand on tiptoe, you gain an inch . . .

Or you can tell yourself it will heal and concentrate on something else.

There was turmoil on the island. People were shouting at one of their number. He stood with his feet planted wide and his hands raised high over his head. The hands held the haft of a spear: a length of wood that might have been a broken oar or a tree sapling, and a leaf-shaped blade poised a few inches above his feet. Poised to strike, but at what? Hands reached to shake his shoulders, and he snarled in an agony different somehow from all the moans around him.

I tried to hear. By now the wordless moaning of the thousands of waders, even my own, had become a background noise, had faded like the sickening smell of boiling blood. I caught disjointed phrases.

"Kill 'em! Kill 'em before—"

"Billy, if you won't do it, let us through!"

"Idiot, you hafta, they'll be all around us in a minute—"

The man with the spear bellowed, "No!"

And the ground seemed to erupt beneath his feet.

He kicked at whatever was gripping his ankles. He kicked himself free and ran for the island's shore. Others got out of his way, then surged to close the gap. Behind him, that portion of the island was heaving as in an earthquake, and clubs and knives were rising and falling with horrible rhythm.

"Billy" splashed knee deep into boiling blood and stopped at once. As he sucked air for his first shocked scream, three separate hands thrust forward against his back. He splashed face down. Two surging waves washed against the bathers around him.

He was up in a flash, his spear ready for war. I was sure he'd try to fight his way back onto the island. But he didn't. He turned and waded away, in our direction. A foot short of my nose he said, "Friend, it's not polite to stare."

"Sorry. What happened back there? Will they let you back?"

He glared back at his erstwhile neighbors. "Those bastards couldn't stop *me*." He sounded like he was holding his breath . . . as we all did, because each of us was trying to talk around a scream. It was almost funny, that sound. "I . . . never thought it would hurt so much," he said.

"Why didn't you stay?"

"Couldn't take the killing."

"What?"

Benito and Corbett had crowded close to listen. "Billy" studied me, his face contorted in agony. "Don't know about the island, do you?"

I shook my head. The Afrika Korps had gone, but cuirassiers with muskets had replaced them. We still dared not move.

"We on the island, we killed people, just like you in the swimming hole. But we all had some excuse, some reason we had to kill. Like me. There was a range war going on. We wasn't even the ones that started it."

I said, "Yeah?"

He took it wrong. "You think maybe we could have stopped it? Gone along with the amnesty?"

I didn't know what he was talking about and didn't much care. His blue eyes had turned killer in that moment. I said, "Don't mind me. I'm in Hell too."

That calmed him, and changed him. He was younger than me and shorter than me, and the short amateurish haircut gave him a pleasant boyish look. Though the hair was plastered down with blood . . . "Then there's Harry Vogel," he continued, "he was robbing a liquor store and the owner pulled his mask off. He'd seen his face, so he had to die, see? And Rich and Bonny Anderson, they kidnapped a kid, and it would have been okay, but he got away. Got as far as a great big street called a freeway, then some kind of machine hit him." He looked down, then continued talking, hurriedly, as if that would block the pain. "Bonny's here, Rich isn't. Rich got religion. Hey, we got Aaron Burr on the island! And that guy who ran the Andersonville prison camp—"

"I get the idea. If they thought they had to do it, they don't get hurt as bad."

"Yeah." Billy looked down a his waist. "It hurts. I think this hurts as much as anything I ever did except die. But I wouldn't go back. No." But he looked back and wasn't sure. He said it again. "No! I won't ever kill anyone again!"

"That's twice you've—"

"Well, that island ain't any common dirt, you know. It's mostly judges and congressmen and lawyers and a few jury members and crooked sheriffs—"

"Wait! Wait!" I remembered the island surging up around him. "The island's people? Live people?"

I swear he was enjoying my reaction. "Yeah. We have to keep 'em crippled. It's what Minos does to them for letting known killers loose on the public that was paying them to protect them. Some was jury members that took bribes, and lawyers that fiddled with the evidence, and congressmen that passed laws against putting a man in jail if the evidence wasn't got in a special kind of way . . . I don't know. That kind of law is all new to me. The island was a lot smaller when I came here."

"And they keep coming back to life!" I was this shocked: I had forgotten to hurt.

"Friend, they sure do. And we have to keep persuading them not to move, one way or another. Otherwise they'd just swim away, and where'd we be?"

"Waist deep in boiling blood?"

He tried to laugh. "Well, I guess I'd rather boil. If they could die it'd be okay, but they can't. Let 'em alone long enough and they try to get up. I can't take it anymore."

I felt Benito's hand on my shoulder. "Allen, the shore is clear of guards. I think we can move."

Corbett was already raising a wake. I started after him, tottering on stiffened legs. On impulse I turned back. "Why not come with us? It can't be any worse lower down."

His eyes sparked with hope. "Maybe you're right."

16

WE WADED THROUGH BOILING BLOOD, GOING UP TO OUR chins before the bottom sloped up again. After an eternity we reached the other shore and let ourselves fall, each wrapped silently and solipsistically in his own pain. We lay in full view on what seemed to be rough white concrete. Four targets. If the guardians wanted us they could have us.

A long time later, Corbett found the strength to roll over. "They're all along the far shore," he reported. "Watching us. Nazis, Indians—"

Benito said, "Never mind. They will not hurt us. They do not bother those who wish to go deeper into Hell."

"That's a relief," said Corbett.

I wasn't so sure, but I held my peace. I inspected my feet, legs, buttocks. The meat was loose on my bones. I should have been dead down there; it should have stopped hurting. *Fat chance, Carpentier.*

And Billy, who must have hurt just as much as I did, was smiling to himself. I snarled, "What are you so damned happy about?"

"First off, this is the first chance I've had to lie down

in a hundred years. Second, I don't have to kill anyone, even if they yell at me. Third, I didn't much like the company on that island. Maybe I'll like you better."

"Maybe. Who were you?"

"William Bonney. Just a cowhand that got done unto and did some back."

"Bonney?" Corbett sat up suddenly. He'd healed much faster than I had. "Billy the Kid?"

"Friend, there are a dozen men on the island that all claim they was Billy the Kid."

"And you?"

"I'm the real one."

I could see the wheels going round in Corbett's head. Were we supposed to spend eternity wondering if he were telling the truth? Corbett said, "Have it your way. I was a spaceship pilot."

"What? You mean like you been on the Moon?"

"Right."

Benito grunted and surged to his feet, then sat down hard with another grunt of pain. From the waist down he showed bright red skin, very tender looking. Like Corbett he'd healed fast, but he wasn't in condition to scout.

I asked, "Benito, what are we headed into? It's for sure we can't go back."

"The Wood of the Suicides lies ahead. A pleasant place, comparatively, if we can avoid the dogs."

"Dogs?"

"The Wood is punishment for the sin of suicide," Benito explained. "Each tree holds the soul of one who took his own life. They are not dangerous to us. But the Violent Wasters also suffer there, and the dogs are their punishment. There will not be many of the dog packs. It is almost an obsolete sin."

Corbett looked up. "Since when is a sin obsolete?"

"Customs change. In Dante's time there were men

who would hold a party at which they would burn part of their wealth, to show how wealthy they were."

"Potlach!" I cried.

"Gesundheit," said Corbett.

"No, dammit, listen. There was a West Coast Indian tribe that used to do just what Benito's talking about. Hold a party, burn a lot of valuables. They used to compete at it. I never knew the Italians did the same thing."

"They did," said Benito. "Their punishment is to run through these woods pursued by wild dogs. If the dogs catch them they tear them apart."

Billy was sitting up. "They heal after *that?*"

I was healing! My legs and buttocks still hurt, but the flesh was firm, and I could move the muscles. I watched, fascinated, as new skin grew before my eyes.

"The dogs and the souls they pursue should be rare," Benito said, "and the trees can do us no harm. We should find this stretch easy." He stood up. "Are we ready?"

My feet were still tender, and Billy was complaining about his. But it didn't sound like we'd have to run anywhere. Corbett and Benito were healed.

We set off, deeper into Hell. It had become an obsession with me. Anything was better than waiting—and if I spent too much time remembering the agony in the lake, we'd *never* get started.

We left concrete for dirt. When we topped a gentle rise, the ground was suddenly all erosion gullies, hard red and yellow clay studded with gravel and gashed by flash floods. We had to scramble in and out of them. Some had water at the bottom, water filthy with broken bottles and bottle caps, used condoms, floating grease, occasional bursts of brightly colored dyes, chemicals that burned our sandaled feet. Nothing grew here; there were dead stumps of trees and dried brown vines reaching upward like dead old women's fingers. Strange smells moved on the air: incongruous whiffs of automobile exhaust, acids, burning oil and rubber.

Billy grunted. "I don't see no trees, Benito. Where'd you put the damn trees?"

"We should have reached the Wood long since. I do not understand. But we must go on."

We scrambled out of the gully and looked downward. We had a vista of Hell.

It looked like Hell on Earth. Nothing grew. We had to shout above a continual racket. In the distance rectangular shadows showed through the gloomy half-light and thick smog. Buildings? Factories?

I said, "Progress has caught up with your woods, Benito."

A clattering sounded nearby, within a cloud of roiling smoke. A woman ran out of the smoke, terror on her face, hair streaming behind her. She wore a torn evening gown with diamond brooch and earrings, high-heeled shoes with jeweled ornaments. She ran holding the skirt high.

Billy shouted and tried to stop her. She dodged him and ran on. The clattering grew louder, and a bulldozer roared out of the smoke. A man ran just ahead of the blade. The 'dozer trailed smoke, and it was gaining on the fugitive. There was no driver.

Billy was in the bottom of the gully, curled up, his head wrapped in his arms. When the monster was past I went down to Billy. He was muttering to himself, and when I touched him he twitched galvanically. He leapt to his feet in fighting stance.

"I was never afraid of no man that ever lived," he said. "But I was scared of that. What was it?"

"Bulldozer. For moving dirt."

Billy stared into the smog, his face wondering. "You could tear down whole mountains with things like that."

"We did," Corbett said. "There's more than one way to be a violent waster."

Billy frowned. "How's that?"

"Pollution. This must be the place for people who ruin the environment." Corbett's face showed his disgust. "They did this to the Earth."

"But who gets chased by them things?"

"Real-estate developers, I guess. Housing-tract speculators. We shouldn't have too much trouble here." Corbett looked at us. "Or do we?"

I'd always been a conservationist myself. If Big Juju's poetic justice ran true to form, I'd be safe enough.

Or would I? Had I fallen by accident? I'd certainly put myself on that window ledge. If a bulldozer buried me here, would I become a tree?

"Let's go," said Billy. "This place gives me the willies."

We moved off by tacit consent.

"Where we going, anyway?" Billy asked.

"Past this round there is desert," Benito said. "A fiery desert, too hot for life, with flame falling from the sky. I know of only one way to cross it, and that is the way Dante used. A stream runs through the desert, the overflow from the lake of blood. It cools the desert as it moves through it."

"Miraculously," I said. I'd intended it to be contemptuous, but it hadn't come out that way. I'd seen too many miracles, all unpleasant.

Benito nodded. "Of course. We must find this stream, or we cannot cross. It runs through the Wood. Comrades, we must find the Wood." He turned left and walked on.

"Why this way?" Billy laughed. "You ain't got any idea where that Wood is."

"No, but we must reach it if we walk far enough. It is only a matter of time."

Yeah, we had plenty of that. And Hell was a series of concentric circles, God only knew how big around. It might take years, and so what?

"Why not go the other way?" Billy insisted.

Benito shrugged. "Dante always turned left on his way down. But we will turn right if you like."

"Naw. It ain't important."

17

THE NOISE, THE SMELLS, THE DESOLATION CONTINUED. The damned were here, placed by a macabre humor. Phantom heads rose from oil pools. Some were pecked incessantly by oil-smeared birds. A river ran past like an open sewer, and men and women lined the banks, mourning. The wails were constant in our ears, wails and roaring motors and clanking machines.

We looked into some of the huge buildings and pulled back out fast. Inside the noise was overwhelming. Here a sizzling hum of electricity, there a scream of metal grinding on metal, elsewhere a roar of flame. There were more of the damned in those buildings, and they were hard at work.

Our way led through one of the immense factories. Not a head lifted to see us pass. Incomprehensible widgets passed on an endless belt, and men and women screwed on nuts and tightened them and fitted the bottoms and the handles, endlessly. We followed the endless belt for miles until it went through a wall. On the other side more of the damned were taking the widgets apart. Machinery hummed, and conveyors took the parts back to the other side of the wall.

We left the building to find oil derricks raising and lowering their heads like giant prehistoric birds. We crossed a strip mine, and Benito pointed out that it was laid out very like Hell itself: a vast series of descending circular terraces. But there was nothing at the bottom except stagnant water.

A towering oil-fueled power plant of spidery framework and miles of pipes and valves poured power into a cable thick as my waist. Transmission towers took the cable downhill.

I peered along its length, but the murk defeated me. How did they use electricity in Hell? But outside the power plant was an athletic man chained to a wheelless bicycle set in concrete in front of the exhaust pipe of the generator. Black smoke poured around him, almost hiding him from view.

As we watched he began pedaling furiously. The hum of the gears rose to a high pitch—and the generator inside died. There was a moment of quiet. The man pedaled with sure strokes, faster and faster, his feet nearly invisible, his head tucked down as if against a wind. We gathered around, each wondering how long he could keep it up.

He began to tire. The blur of his feet slowed. The motors inside coughed, and black smoke poured out. He choked and turned his head away, and saw us.

"Don't answer if you'd rather not," I said, "but what whim of fate put you here?"

"I don't *know!*" he howled. "I was president of the largest and most effective environmental protection organization in the country! I *fought* this!" He braced himself and pedaled again. The hum rose, and the generator died.

Billy was completely lost. He looked to Benito, but our guide only shrugged. Benito accepted everything. I knew better. This couldn't be justice, not even Big Juju's exaggerated justice. This was monstrous.

Corbett had to be guessing when he suddenly asked, "You opposed thermonuclear power plants?"

The guy stopped dead, staring as if Corbett were a ghost. The dynamo lurched into action and surrounded him with thick blue smoke.

"That's it, isn't it?" Corbett said gently. "You stopped the nuclear generators. I was just a kid during the power blackouts. We had to go to school in the dark because the whole country went on daylight saving time to save power."

"But they weren't safe!" He coughed. "They weren't safe!"

"How did you know that?" Benito asked.

"We had scientists in our organization. They proved it."

We turned away. Now I knew. I could quit looking for justice in Hell. There was only macabre humor. Why should that man be in the inner circles of Hell? At worst he belonged far above, with the bridge-destroyers of the second ledge. Or in Heaven. *He* hadn't created this bleak landscape.

I couldn't stand it. I went back. Benito shrugged and motioned to the others.

Within the cloud of blue smoke his face was slack with exhaustion. "It wasn't just the problem of where to bury the waste products," he told me. "There was radioactive gas going into the air." He spoke as if continuing a conversation. I must have been his only audience in years, or decades.

"You got a rotten deal," I said. "I wish I could do something."

He smiled bravely. "What else is new?" And he started to pedal.

I glared at the nothing sky, hating Big Juju. *Carpentier declares war*. When I looked down, Benito was fumbling through saddlebags attached to the stationary bicycle.

The man cried, "What are you doing?"

Benito took out papers. The man snatched at them, but Benito backed away. He read, "Dear Jon, I could understand your opposition to us last year. There was some doubt about the process, and you expressed fears all of us felt. But now you know better. I have no witnesses, but you told me you understood Dr. Pittman's demonstration. In God's name, Jon, why do you continue? I ask you as your sister, as a fellow scientist, as a human being: why?"

He began pedaling again, ignoring us.

"You knew?" I demanded. He pedaled faster, his head bent. I leaned down and put my face close to his. "You knew?" I screamed.

"Fuck off."

Big Juju wins again. Too much, but appropriate. As we walked away, Jon screamed after us, "I'd have been *nothing* if I gave up the movement! Nothing! Don't you understand? I had to stay as president!"

We plunged on. Once we caught lungfuls of something unidentifiable. We were getting used to that by now. This time we wound up at the bottom of an erosion gully, kicking and twitching, unable to control our muscles.

"N-n-nerve g-g-gas," said Corbett.

We lay there for hours. Days perhaps. Eventually the wind shifted, and our legs could work again. Benito and Corbett scrambled up the side of the gully, then came back for Billy and me. As usual we were the last to heal. Big Juju's biological engineers hadn't done as good a job on us. We scrambled to the top.

Beyond the gully we saw trees.

That was all we could see through the sniffles and the tears and the dark, smoky air: a sharply bordered forest, some distance away.

We began to run. Trees. Real living things! or close to it; nothing was really alive in this terrible place. But trees! We ran, wearing fierce grins, noses lifted as if the air were already sweet . . .

Closer, they were not so inviting. Gnarled trunks, black leaves . . . Not Mother Nature herself could have called them pretty. Clumsy birds flapped above them. The forest ended abruptly at a border of flat ground. No, not ground. I stopped at the edge, confused.

The others ran heedlessly out onto the flat black borderland.

It was a road. Blacktop, and a white double line down the center. I called, "Hey, wait a . . ."

Things roared past and drowned my voice. Too fast to tell what they were, but I knew the sound: the whip of air, followed by a shriek of brakes. I screamed, "Run!"

Corbett was already running for his life. Benito and Billy stared at me; then Benito just took my word for it and ran toward me. Billy looked where I was looking . . . and for him it was already too late.

They looked like black Corvettes, 1970's models, but they were lower-slung and more rakish-looking. They'd stopped and turned and were coming back, accelerating hugely, leaving opaque black clouds of smoke. Billy made up his mind to run; he turned, and they were on him. Billy flew high, hit hard, and rolled like a beanbag: no bones.

I started swearing. The cars roared away . . . two of them did. The third turned hard, right off the road. It rolled over once and landed upright and came for us, bouncing and rattling, but accelerating. Its headlights came on blindingly.

I stopped swearing and looked for cover.

"What are they?" Benito screamed.

"Cars. No drivers," Corbett told him. "I saw. Empty race cars. They must guard the forest."

I looked for cover: something to hide behind, or even a jumble of broken rock too rough for a car. Nothing. The black demon bore down on us.

"There!" I pointed, and ran. It was an oil slick, depth unknown, and it would bloody well have to do.

I ran straight into the pool. My foot landed on something that jerked away and sent me sprawling. When I pulled my face out of the oil another black, dripping face looked back at me. "Sorry," I said.

"That's okay. We all got our own problems here," said the stranger, and he sank beneath the oil.

Benito was waist deep and wading deeper. Corbett hesitated at the edge, looked disgusted, looked behind him . . . squealed and dived sideways. I ducked under. The glare of headlights was branded on my closed eyes.

A wave of oil splashed over me. I lifted my head, and there it was: a rakish black sports car, hubcap-deep in the oil pool. Its motor was a demon-snarl; its wheels spun frantically. It found some traction from somewhere: it edged backward, found more traction and surged out of the pool just as Corbett went over the door in a flying dive.

The horn screamed in rage. The car backed, then turned in a tight circle. I think it was trying to roll over. It never made it. The motor died, the killer car rolled to a gentle stop.

Corbett stood up in the driver's seat, grinning all over his face. The keys dangled from his hand.

Benito and I waded out, streaming oil.

Corbett had the hood of the murder car up and was inspecting the motor. "I used to race a little," he said. "I can probably drive this. What do you say, shall we cross the desert in comfort?"

"You look it over," I told him. Benito and I went to see about Billy.

He lay twisted as no living man could be. We straightened him out. His body was mushy and limp. So was one side of his head. The good eye opened and looked at us.

Benito bent over Billy and took one of his hands between his own. "I don't know if you can hear me," he said. "I want you to know that you will heal. It will hurt, but you will heal."

I beckoned Benito out of Billy's hearing. I asked, "Should we take him with us?"

"I think so. He will be of no help until he heals, but what of that? He should be safe enough in an automobile. He can ride in the passenger seat."

We rejoined Corbett at the car.

"I don't know the make," he told us. "It's got a big mill, but the tuning is lousy. You saw how much smoke it was pouring out. I've been checking the brakes, and they look good—"

"The question," said Benito, "is whether it will obey the steering wheel and other controls. We saw it driving itself."

"Yeah." Corbett frowned, studying the car as one would search the face of a prisoner of war. Would he give information? Would it be the truth? "The top's down. We can always jump clear," he said. "No point in taking chances, though. Why don't you two get under cover, and I'll take her for a spin."

There wasn't any cover. We stood at the far edge of the oil pool, ready to jump, as Corbett turned the ignition key. He drove the car around for a while, trying it on rough and smooth terrain. He brought it back and prudently took the key before he got out.

"Seems okay. I'll stay in low gear the whole trip. That way nothing can happen fast. If the gearshift starts moving by itself I'll give a yell."

"There's one more problem," I said. "Four of us. Two seats. Benito, shall we ride on the fenders?"

"I have no better suggestion."

The change was gradual. The air got hotter. Then there were no more oil pools. The dead ground gave way to hot dead sand, and Corbett worried aloud about the tires. A minute later he'd forgotten the tires; he was too busy slapping away fat flakes of burning matter.

18

IT SNOWED FIRE. GREAT BURNING FLAKES FELL slowly from the dead gray sky and settled on us. We slapped frantically. Billy was slumped like a corpse while fireflakes dropped to his skin and clung. I could reach his head by stretching backward along the fender, and I pulled a saucer-sized chunk from his face. His one good eye thanked me.

We rolled across a burning sandy waste. The fireflakes vanished when they touched ground, but not when they touched flesh. Another evil miracle. The car weaved drunkenly, then shifted into second and picked up speed.

I called back to Corbett. "Did you do that?"

"Yeah! You want to be out here forever?"

"Not really." The sand was flat enough for higher speed—provided we could control the car.

Billy grunted in soft protest. I could imagine his fear. He'd never seen a car before or gone faster than a horse could run.

Fire bored into my back where I'd exposed it

stretching to help Billy again. I slapped it off and wished for a Cadillac.

Cadillacs *belong* in Hell. There's something about the car that rots the driver's brain. Every time some damn fool has almost gotten me wrecked by running a red light or jumping lanes or parking where no car ought to be, said idiot has been driving a Cadillac. There *had* to be Cadillacs in Hell—and if we'd captured one of those, we'd be riding in air-conditioned comfort! Instead of riding a fender and slapping fire-flakes!

Clusters of souls danced frenetically on the blazing sand. Some stopped, amazed, to watch us pass. A couple of times Corbett tooted the horn at them. He was cursed for his trouble, but he wasn't mocking them. There was nothing he could do.

I called across the low hood to Benito. "Who are they?"

Benito was busy tearing burning gunk out of his hair. "They sinned against Nature," he yelled back.

"What does that mean?"

"Unnatural love. Man for man, woman for woman—"

Man for sheep, woman for vibrator . . . poor bastards. I wondered about the gay couple who'd owned the house next door to mine. Quiet neighbors, friendly middle-aged people like any married couple without children. Were they here?

I turned my head and hunched up so that the fire-flakes hit the side of my face instead of the front. I couldn't slap fast enough. The windshield gave Billy some protection now that we were moving.

The fire burned holes in my skin. *You'll heal, Carpentier. You'll heal, if we ever get out of here.*

But what about them? They danced, they slapped at themselves; they ran in circles; they screamed at us to stop and cursed us when we didn't, with an insane jealousy that I understood perfectly. They'd be here forever.

This, just for being queer? But it was no surprise to me that God's justice and mine didn't agree. I thought about my neighbors and shuddered. *Credo in un Dio crudel . . .*

The industrial section of Hell was only a yellow tinge to the sky behind us. Ahead was nothing but more desert. We must be about halfway across, I thought.

Suddenly the car surged forward with the bit in its teeth.

Corbett froze in panic. The motor screamed in inhuman fury as the car accelerated. In a second we'd be moving too fast to stop. I tucked my head in my arms and rolled off the fender.

Look, I wasn't running out on my buddies. The car was going to crash, and they'd have a better chance if one of us could move, right? It was what I was thinking, anyway.

The motor choked off while I was still in the air.

I hit rolling. I came up screaming and dancing. The other souls hadn't been dancing for joy either. The pain was as bad as the boiling blood.

The car rolled to a stop, and I ran for it, yelling and swearing at the fireflakes.

Suddenly a girl was running alongside me. She'd have been pretty once. Now her hair was raggedly scorched, and her body was covered with burns. "Can you take me out of here?" She screamed.

"We'll be lucky to get out ourselves. There's no room!" I kept running until I reached the car.

The girl stayed right with me. "Please, I'll do anything if you'll take me out of here. *Anything.*"

"That's nice," Corbett told her. To me he said,

"We're in big trouble. The gas pedal just damned well floored itself. I had to turn off the ignition."

"Couldn't you—"

"Couldn't I what? Pull the pedal up with my toes? Allen, this car is haunted. It hates us."

"What's wrong?" the girl asked. She got no answer.

It was hard to think with the fire settling on me. I danced around the car, shouting, "We'd better think of something. In a minute or two we'll be under a pyramid of people." The damned were running toward us from all directions.

"Raise the bonnet," Benito commanded. "Corbett, see to Billy."

I got the hood up. We looked inside, and Benito said, "Now, Corbett, move the accelerator."

Something wiggled behind the engine.

"Allen, you saw? That moves the petrol feed. You must control it with your fingers."

It was a hell of an awkward position, sprawled across the fender with my head and hands under the hood. The motor was as hot as the sand. I couldn't avoid touching it. But I pulled at the widget and cried, "Okay! I got it! Corbett, go! Go like a bat!" The crowd was very near, and they couldn't *all* hang on. Benito motioned to the girl, and she took the fender in front of me.

The car roared and surged into a converging circle. Most of them dodged for their lives. One went under the wheels. Another, a big athletic type with long black hair halfway down his back and a scraggly beard, got the edge of the right door and swung up on the trunk lid. A small-boned blond man had come with him. "Frank!" the companion called. "Frank! Don't leave me!"

"Sorry, Gene. Nothing I can do. No room for both of us."

"Frank!" The car gunned ahead as Corbett got it under control again. A thin voice followed us. "Frank! I went to Hell for you . . ."

Frank had managed to crawl up to get an arm around Corbett's neck. He squeezed. "All right, buddy, turn this thing around! We're going to Havana!"

"Fine. Whatever you say," said Corbett. Frank grinned and slacked off his grip on Corbett, but he didn't let go.

Now we had Frank on the trunk; Billy in the passenger seat, groaning a little, still unable to move; Benito on the left front fender; me in the motor compartment trying to stay clear of the hot engine, my legs dangling out to the right; and the girl forward on the right front fender, her feet on the bumper. Corbett had his problems driving. He had to lean way out to the left to see around the open hood.

Billy was able to scream now.

"For God's sake, brush the fire off him, Frank!" Corbett yelled.

"Screw that. Screw God too. Get moving."

We moved. Corbett yelled, and I slacked off on the gas to let him shift to second. That was fast enough. The car fought, the hot metal tugged against my fingers like something alive, but I could control the speed. At least we weren't hitting any bumps.

"Heeehaaah!" Frank screamed in joy. "Better'n the last chicken run! I'll make you guys honorary Hell's Angels! We're tough, you know? Toughest bunch in the world, you know? Hick sheriff was so scared of us he called the state fuzz. We run for it. I had the lead. Come around a curve and the whole road was full of fuzzmobiles. I got two fuzz smearing myself."

"Your friend back there—" I shouted.

"Gene? We did some swinging times, man. Had a whole stable of 'em. Boys, girls, but the only one

they let me keep here was Gene. Maybe I'll miss him."
He didn't look back.

"Could you get that fire off my leg?" I asked the
girl.

"Naw! Enough trouble holding on here."

"You said you'd do anything!" I clenched my teeth
in agony. There was fire on both legs now, and I
couldn't slap. I couldn't let go of the spring, and I had
to hold on with the other hand. The car was still fighting me. "Get that fire off or we'll throw you off!"

"Awright, awright, you don't have to get nasty."
She slapped a couple of times and got the worst away.

"Who are you?" Benito asked.

"Doreen Lancer," she yelled above the roaring
motor. "Go-go dancer. One night some bastard raped
me and strangled me. At least, he tried to rape me!"
She laughed bitterly. "He didn't seem to know how to
go about it!"

"So what the hell are you doing here?" Frank demanded.

"Don't know! I liked it every which way. Most of
the types I meet here are fags—"

"I'm no goddamn fag!" Frank yelled.

"Do not blaspheme," Benito told him, predictably,
I guess.

"Fuck off! Talk to me that way and I'll twist this
bastard's neck off!" The car lurched as he choked Corbett.

"No!" Doreen screamed. "We'll crash! This is our
only way out! Leave him alone—Look, don't hurt him,
and when we get out we can really swing, right?"

I laughed. I couldn't help it.

"What's so funny?" she demanded.

"It's not a romantic situation!" I bellowed. I wasn't
even sure there could be sex in Hell, and I hadn't
found any opportunity to try. Or inclination, either.

I bellowed again when she slapped my testicles. It hurt as much as it had when I was alive. I pulled the accelerator widget out, tugging with all my strength, letting the car slow.

"I'm sorry!" she yelled. "I was getting the fire off, I swear, that's all I was doing! I'm sorry . . . hey, you wanna be a threesome with Frank and me?"

I let the car speed up again. We had to get out of here. But I'd never had an offer I liked less.

"I can see something ahead!" Corbett shouted. "We're getting to the edge!"

"About time," Frank said. We rolled on. "Just remember, pretty boy, I'm in charge here," he added, and Corbett grunted in pain. Frank must have emphasized his words.

The horizon was sharp ahead. I could barely see over the motor. Corbett saw it too. "Kill the power!" he yelled. Brakes screeched, and he twisted the wheel hard.

I climbed out of the motor. The fireflakes were thicker here than in the middle of the desert. We ran, hopping—

Frank still had Corbett by the neck. "This the way out of here? What are you trying to pull?"

There was a sheer drop ahead of us. It was gloomy down there. I couldn't see the bottom. Several hundred feet, anyway. "Now what?" I asked Benito.

"The quick way would be to jump." He was dead serious. "Jump and wait to heal, then go on."

The girl backed away, staring at him. "You're crazy! Crazy! I should have known better than to trust guys like you! All the promises you make—" She didn't finish, but ran back into the desert, crying.

"That's done it!" Frank yelled. "You're sure as Hell going over that cliff, all right, because I'm going to throw you!" He had Corbett by the neck, and he dragged him toward the cliff edge. "First you, then your loudmouth friend, then the fat one, and then—"

He'd forgotten Billy. We all had. It was a mistake for Frank. Billy launched himself from the car without warning. He landed on Frank's back and seized the long hair with one hand, pulled the head back, and wrapped his arm around Frank's neck. His knee gouged into the Hell's Angel's back, bowing him into an arc. "Friend, I don't think I like you."

I yelled, "Billy! Are you all right?"

"Yeah."

"You weren't moving—"

"Been able to move awhile now. Didn't seem like a good idea to let this creep know it. Jerry coulda crashed this thing if we were fightin' while it was movin'."

I thought about the self-control it would take to sit still under a rain of sticky fire.

"What'll I do with the Gila monster, Benito?"

"Leggo! I was only kidding!" Frank yelled. "You guys got no business giving me false hopes! It was all your fault—" He stopped talking because Billy's arm had closed his throat.

"Do not harm him," Benito said quietly.

"Yeah?" Billy let him go. "Friend, you're not tough. You don't know what tough is. Now get away from us." The pale-blue eyes seemed infinitely deep, and cold even in this place of fire.

"You may come with us if you like," Benito told Frank, "although I do not think you are ready. With your attitude you might well find a worse place than you have now. Still, you are welcome to join us."

"Go to Hell!" Frank screamed. He thought that was funny. "Go to Hell! Go to Hell!" He ran away into the desert, laughing, screaming, trying to keep both feet off the hot sand at once.

Benito looked at us, waiting.

"I'll jump if you say so," Billy said. "Looks bad, though. I can tell you, being crushed flat ain't no fun."

I gulped. "I will too." I wondered if I meant it.

"There may be a better way," Benito said. "We must find the stream. Corbett, can you drive?"

"Sure."

We turned left. I had the whole fender to sprawl on now. The car seemed more docile, too, but I wasn't going to trust it. I didn't really have to—I was getting good at manipulating the gas widget.

We came to a horde of people dressed in the finery of all ages: velvet robes, flare pants, alligator shoes. Corbett shouted at me. "Stopping!" He turned off the key before I could do anything, and the car rolled to a halt.

Fireflakes fell on us. "Now what?"

Corbett was out of the car and looking at a beefy man in gaudy tunic, crimson sash, and black glove-leather boots. There was a big leather wallet hung on a golden chain around his neck, and he stared into it, not looking up. The fireflakes had burned holes in his tunic and scorched his hair.

Corbett stood in front of him. When the burly man didn't look up, Corbett stooped over so that his face was in line with the wallet. "Give me my money!" Corbett shouted.

"You son of a bitch, you owe *me!*"

"But I've had this problem, see, my girl is . . ." Corbett began.

"I don't want to hear any stories, I just want my money! Arrgh!" A big fireflake settled on the crown of his head. He tried to brush it off.

"Hang tough," Corbett said. He came back to the car chuckling. "Long Harry there loaned me some cash, once. Six for five—every week."

I nodded. There were lots of others there, crying into their purses. The rain of fire seemed heavier here. "Let's get going." I didn't like Corbett gloating over them—but if anybody deserved to be here, it was them. Loan shark is as low a form of life as there is.

We didn't drive so fast that we couldn't talk. "Funny thing about Harry," Corbett said. "He had to give up the loan shark business. Had a customer with a hit man for a friend. Took his buddy Lem to see Harry, but Harry wouldn't listen. Just kept saying 'Give me my money.' So Lem had a talk with Harry."

"Lem?" Billy asked. He sounded puzzled.

"Yeah. I don't know what he told Harry, but just after that all of Harry's customers were off the hook. Just had to pay what they'd got in the first place."

"Lem," Billy said. "Little guy? About my size? Big scar over his left eye?"

"Yeah," Corbett said. "You know him?"

"Kind of. They used to let him onto the island for a day. One day a year. The rest of the time he was out in the blood. I always did wonder why."

"We are coming to the stream," Benito said. "The fire does not fall there."

19

THE RIVER WAS NARROW BUT FAST. ITS ROAR WAS different somehow from that of water, and it was still bright scarlet. The air was thick with the smell of blood.

Nonetheless we walked down and bathed our half-broiled feet in it. Afterward we walked the cool mud of the bank with our sandals off until we reached the waterfall. There we watched endless tons of blood falling into the darkness.

I said, "Now what?"

Benito scowled in indecision. "It is a risk. The monster Geryon carried Dante and Vergil into lower Hell. But they were on a holy errand. We are not. I have known Geryon. He is not worthy of trust."

"The password," I remembered.

" 'This has been willed where what is willed must be.' Yes. Shall we try it?"

"Better'n jumping." Billy looked at Benito. "It is, ain't it? What can he do to us? Eat us?"

"Summon Minos."

155

"Let's try it," said Corbett. "We've gotten this far without anyone doing that."

"Are we agreed, then? Good. Now we must summon Geryon. We need a signal, something to get his attention. Dante flung a rope into the abyss."

"A signal," said Corbett. "Does it have to be subtle?"

"I should not think that subtlety would be necessary."

"We wouldn't want Geryon to think we're crude, would we? Some delicate change in the environment, just noticeable enough to attract his attention. Let me see." Corbett walked back to the car and switched on the ignition. He went around to the back and unscrewed the gas cap.

A fireflake fell past his nose. He blew on it, guiding it into the gas tank. The tank lit with a *whoosh*. Hurriedly Corbett reached into the car and shifted it into first gear. We stood well back and watched it roll over the edge.

"Subtlety is all," said Corbett.

The car fell like a battlefield flare. It passed and illuminated a compact body already rising through the murk.

"He knew we were here." Corbett was flat on his belly with his face over the cliff's edge. "We didn't need a signal."

"He will not come without a signal," said Benito.

The car was a towering flame at the base of the cliff. Lighted from below, Geryon was a compact shadow with a slender, twisting tail. He floated up to us, his features growing clear. He hovered at our height, smiled reassuringly at us with a startlingly human face, then slid forward onto the rock ledge, leaving his tail hanging free in space.

Geryon was as big as a rowboat, and wingless. His

hind feet were webbed, built for swimming. His almost human head was hairless, the mouth wide, the chin broad and strong, the nose very wide and flat, with large nostrils. The head sloped back to round shoulders, without benefit of neck.

His arms were human enough, the size of my own. On Geryon they were disproportionately small. Something was funny about the hand: the fingers were short and thick, designed for ripping.

I could see him as an air-breathing aquatic beast that had developed human intelligence. I wondered about his nose. It was big enough to feed him air fast, hooded to keep water out. Reasonable, but different from the cetacean design.

His pelt had the look of medieval tapestry: golden knots and figures on a blue-gray background. Lovely; a trifle flashy. And adequate camouflage if he was used to hovering just beneath sunlit water.

Altogether he was a believable alien, excluding his ability to fly. I didn't like that. Bad enough if Infernoland had been built by humans. What if it had been built by interstellar conquerors for their own amusement?

Geryon's voice was deep, with a queer buzzing quality. "Hello, Benito. Three of them? Isn't that a bit much?"

Benito was brusque. He didn't like Geryon. "This has been willed where what is willed must be. In any case, you must have noticed how the damned flow in like a river in flood—"

"Haven't I just. Swamping you, are they? I think the end of the world must be near. Hell is getting full," said the alien. "Well, we who serve God's will in Hell have precious little of free will, eh, Benito? Climb aboard, you. I hope you all can hang on."

He had spoken jovially, with no bitterness and only the merest trace of mockery.

My foot kicked something rigid as I tried to board Geryon's reasonably flat back. I looked down. It wasn't easy to see, but there was metal belted about Geryon's belly, machinery covered with material the same color as his gaudy pelt.

Antigravity?

I settled behind the monster's head. Billy's arms closed about my waist. Corbett was behind him, and Benito last, braving the twin stings in the forked tail. Geryon grinned at me over his shoulder and pushed back from the edge.

Billy's arms tightened convulsively. I saw that his eyes were closed tight, his teeth clenched.

My view of Hell was darkness and firelit smokes, the fires tracing concentric arcs. Geryon tilted to one side and dropped in a slow spiral. The scarlet water-fall dashed itself to foam and spray on the rocks. Billy was squeezing the breath from me, but I didn't complain. I heard whimpering noises being squeezed from him.

We touched down.

I said, "Your first flight, Billy?"

"Yeah."

"We're down. You can let go."

"Yeah." He unlocked his arms in stages and climbed down on shaky legs. I followed.

Geryon floated up a few feet and hovered. "Hey, Benito," he called. His voice was full of artificial camaraderie, more menacing than threats. "Why is it, Benito, that the people you travel with don't ever come back?" The monster lifted toward the sky, chortling.

Carefully casual, Corbett asked Benito, "You've been here before?"

"I have rescued others," Benito answered.

"How many?"

"Six. One at a time. No matter how many come with me at first, no more than one at a time ever seems to reach the exit point. Perhaps this time we will be more fortunate."

"What happens to the others?" I asked.

"Why did you come back?" Corbett demanded.

We'd both spoken at once, and Benito chose to answer neither of us.

"Have you seen the exit?" Corbett asked.

Benito's voice was colorlessly grim. "Yes."

"And gone beyond it?"

"No. But it follows Dante's route, which leads to Purgatory. I came back to find others in need of guidance. Do *you* object, Allen Carpentier? Should I have left you in the bottle?"

"Hey, hey, hey!" Billy was dancing with impatience. "If we're going, let's *go!* What's all the jawing about?"

Benito nodded and led us off downslope. We felt exposed on level ground, and Geryon couldn't be the only flying thing. He hadn't reported us (had he?), but that was no guarantee that something else wouldn't. We moved swiftly across what seemed to be solid rock, always downhill, further into murk and gloom, until we came to a cliff edge.

There was a ditch in front of us, seventy or eighty feet deep and perhaps twice that wide. It was divided in the middle by a low wall of rock. Just off to our left was a passageway in the dividing rock wall. The divider was low enough that we could see over it, lower than the height of a normal man—

—and the ditch was full. Masses of humanity moved in a standard traffic pattern, all hurrying along, not quite running, leftbound on the far side, rightward on the near side. They moved *fast*.

They moved fast because there were beings with

whips urging them along. It took a moment for that to register.

Okay, Carpentier, you're in Hell and there are demons in Hell. There were things on the red-hot wall that might have been demons if you could have seen them clearly through the fog. There's Geryon, certainly a monster. *Of course* Big Juju can make demons.

But I hadn't wanted to believe it.

Now I was looking at them. They were blackskinned rather than the red I'd expected, and they were at least ten feet tall. They had horns and tails and were uglier than I could have imagined. They used whips twice as long as themselves. They screamed at the laggards:

"Along with you, Big Morris, there's no ass to sell here!"

"Git along, little dogie, git along, git along . . ."

Wails and groans rose from the pit, and screams of pain and rage. Snap! Crack! Chunks of flesh flew from the backs of those who slowed down.

"Who . . ." whispered Corbett. He ran out of voice and had to try again. "Who are they?" He was frightened, and why not? I was scared out of my mind. The demons were looking up at us—

—but they went back to their tasks, gleefully lashing the crowd. I recognized one of the runners. He was a famous movie director-producer, idolized by millions when I was younger. He was on the near side, but as he reached the passageway in the dividing wall the demon stationed there lashed him until he went through and joined those scurrying in the other direction.

I'd never met him, but I knew who he was. And I knew who these people must be.

Benito confirmed my suspicions. "Panderers on this side, seducers on the other. Come, we must find a bridge." He turned left, and we followed uncertainly.

"I . . . was a seducer," Corbett said uncertainly.

I remembered the convention atmosphere and what happened the night before I died. "Me too."

Benito snorted. "Did you ever have a woman against her will?"

"No—"

"Or make her drunk, or drug her?"

"Well—" Did pot count? "Nobody who didn't know what to expect."

"Never had to," Corbett said matter-of-factly.

"Or use threats of force?"

"Don't be silly." Corbett resented the implication. "I told you, it wasn't necessary."

"The Italian does not properly translate as your English seducer, which is hardly more than casual fornication," Benito said seriously. "I think perhaps the better word is 'rape.' "

Now we could see the bridge ahead of us: a stone arch. It looked very old.

"Jerry!" A voice called from the pit. "Jerry! Come on down, Jerry. You *belong* here!"

It stopped Corbett cold. He looked down into the pit. "Julia?"

"Come on down, Jerry. Share *everything* with me. You taught me how, Jerry—"

"How can a girl be a rapist?" I demanded. She was, or had been, quite pretty, but now her face was distorted by pain and exhaustion. The demons were watching her stand there as she panted and shouted up to Corbett, and they didn't interfere.

"Deceit. Fraud," said Benito. "Those who induce others to what they know is wrong, as well as those who force their will on others."

I turned to Corbett and *Shut up, Carpentier! None of your business* closed my mouth.

"You taught me everything, Jerry," she was calling.

"I could still love you. Come down with me. Where else can you go now?"

"Out! Down to the center and out!" Corbett screamed to her.

The demons howled maniac laughter. The girl laughed with them. "Oh, Jerry, do you *believe* that? Don't you know that the deeper you go, the worse it is, and you can't *ever* go back, and you can't get out? It's worse down there, Jerry. Wait till you see who's below us! Here you have *me,* Jerry. Stay where you belong. There's no escape down there. Don't you know what's carved on the gates of Hell, Jerry? All hope abandon!"

"I'm not afraid of what's below!" Corbett was getting hysterical. "I never did any of the things they punish you down there for—"

She laughed again. "The only perfect man who ever lived! Are you *sure,* Jerry? Then why do they let you *go* there? And what makes you think you'll get justice anyway? Come down with me before its too late to—HYEEEE!"

The demons had called time on her. Crack! Snap! The whips sounded like popcorn popping. Julia sprinted, screaming with the rest. The flesh of my back rippled. I wanted to shut my ears.

"Come." Benito took Corbett's arm. "Come. Do not let her seduce you again."

"Uh?" Corbett looked at Benito as if he'd only just met him. "It did happen that way, now you mention it. Or did it? Maybe I do belong in that pit."

"If you do, you will be there. For the moment you are not. Ergo—come along."

We walked in silence, each wrapped in its own thoughts. What if the girl was right? Were we plunging deeper and deeper, never to return? What was below us? Had I committed any of the appropriate crimes? "Benito, what's ahead?"

His dry lecture voice couldn't mask the screaming as we walked the rim. "No more!" "Not again!" "Wait, I'm in the wrong place!" "It was just *one* book, just one. *I needed the money!*" "You big ugly sonofabitch, you—" *Crack!*

"Of the ten *bolgias*—canyons—of this circle of Hell, this is the only divided one. Each canyon is crossed by a bridge, except that all the bridges are down across the sixth canyon. We must descend into it. It will be no problem."

"Benito, how in God's name can you ignore those screams?" Corbett demanded.

"They have no more than they deserve," Benito said simply. Either he hadn't the empathy of a turtle, or . . . or what? "Now, we will have trouble at the fifth *bolgia*. It is the pit of grafters, and the demons are on the rim, not down in the canyon."

"Ugh." I'd forgotten most of the Inferno, but I could never have forgotten that image: a troop, an army of devils, ill-mannered and sadistic, a military organization of ugly hate. They'd almost got Dante despite his safe-conduct. "What's after this circle?"

We had reached an arching bridge of rough stone. It had no handrails and was about ten feet wide, a slender arch above that pit of screaming runners. It sloped up so steeply that I dropped to all fours to climb.

"Jerry! Come down, Jerry!" It was the girl again. Corbett stiffened.

"What's next?" I prompted Benito. "After the ten canyons what will we find?"

"Very little," Benito answered. "The great ice plain, where traitors are punished. Those who betrayed their blood kin or their benefactors."

"Not me," Corbett said. He seemed to feel better. "And then?"

"We cross to the very center. There is a hole. We crawl through it, past the center of the world, and find ourselves climbing up again."

"And I can believe as much of that as I like?"

"Certainly. Why should you not believe it?" Benito was genuinely puzzled.

"It's nonsense," said Corbett. "We'd be in free-fall by the time we got there."

"Jerry!"

Corbett shuddered. The voice floated upward again. "Don't be a fool, Jerry. It's bad down there at the center. And they *never* let you out."

"Did I really put her there?" Corbett wondered. "Maybe I have betrayed a benefactor. She was kind to me and—"

"Come on, no woman's worth what they're gettin'," Billy said. "We stick together. I never let a buddy down in my life, and I'm goin' down to the center. Now come on."

Corbett lost some of his tension. "If you're really Billy the Kid, that's right. At least, that's what the movies showed." He began moving again, over the arch of the bridge and downward. "Benito, your description is still nonsense. Not only would there be free-fall at the center of the Earth, but this isn't Earth to begin with. A cavity this size, under the Earth? Can you imagine the *pressures?* And we'd get seismograph readings on it with every earthquake. No, we have to be somewhere else."

"Sure," I said. "Infernoland. Somebody built it, following Dante. But the geography's been the same as the Inferno all the way so far, so what do we care if it's an artifact?"

"It is an artifact," Benito said, "in the sense that God designed and built it."

"Okay," said Corbett. "I was never a good atheist. Not a churchman either. Still, Benito, I've seen designs for bigger structures than this. Bigger than Earth, for that matter. Our real problem is, did Dante really see this place himself? And can we trust his reports?"

That was a good question, but I had a better one. How far could we trust Benito? He had never mentioned earlier trips.

Just how did Benito get back uphill after those trips? How did he earn this privilege of running free through Hell? Geryon had said "we" when speaking of both himself and Benito. "We who serve God's will in Hell."

Benito was an unlikely angel . . . and Geryon an untrustworthy witness, I reminded myself. But this was the Devil's realm, and Benito wandered at whim.

All right, Carpentier: just what *is* the punishment for a soul who defies God's final command? God or Big Juju, I had plenty of evidence that He was vindictive. He put me in the Vestibule, and I violated my sentence. Minos warned me. Is this the final retribution against Carpentier? To go even deeper into Hell, with no way back, to find my own level and have it worse than He condemned me to?

Or. Suppose this really is Infernoland, a bigger and more powerful Builder's playground. Why would the Geryon-type engineers have built anything *but* the Inferno? They clearly enjoyed seeing humans suffer. Would they get a similar kick from human pleasure? All the professors told me the *Inferno* was by far the most interesting of the three books of *The Divine Comedy*.

Benito was talking again. "I have always assumed that Dante made his trek in a vision. When he woke he had forgotten many of the details. He filled them in with research in theology and dogma and philosophy and natural history and with his own whims and prejudices and special hatreds. But the basic vision was sound and true. Be careful here."

The bridge dropped steeply at the end. The inner rim of the trench was twenty feet lower than the outer. We went down backward. The lip of another pit was a hundred yards away. A cacaphony of sound rose from it. We stopped for a moment.

"For instance," Benito said, "Dante's work gives the impression that he met large numbers of Italians—"

"Sounds perfectly reasonable to me," said Corbett. We tried to laugh, but this wasn't a place for laughing.

Benito merely continued as if he hadn't heard. "Improbable numbers of Italians. Large numbers of famous ancients. He met writers, poets, politicians, but no Hottentots, Eskimos, Askaris, or American Indians. This seems unlikely."

"Then you don't trust Dante after all?"

"Jerry, that was not my point."

I said, "Benito, we've met an embarrassing sufficiency of Americans."

Billy laughed. "Plenty on the island, too."

Benito was startled. "It's true. And Hilda Kroft and I met Germans. And—"

"Man tends to notice his own folks," said Billy. "Let's get moving."

We angled toward a bridge spanning the next ditch. Benito still looked disturbed. Why? *That* disturbed *me.*

The smell stopped us joltingly at the second pit. It was like being dropped into a sewer. We didn't even try to look over the edge.

"Who's down there?" Billy asked.

"Flatterers," Benito said shortly, and turned toward the bridge.

We followed. "I don't get it," Corbett said.

"In every place of power, throughout all time, the rulers have been surrounded by flatterers. In many places flattery has been the path to power and wealth. In others it is only a good living. Yet everywhere the flatterers tend to push aside the men of real wisdom. Flattery is so much safer than telling unpleasant truths."

"Not in America," said Corbett.

"This I doubt," said Benito. "But you should know best."

"Never buttered up the boss? I sure have," said Billy.

I felt uncomfortable. What was I doing at the moment I died but flattering the fans? I glanced over at Corbett, and he looked no better. Flattery? We'd all tried it. What did they do to flatterers?

We clustered at the bridge approach and stood looking at it. The smell was thick as putty. I could feel it clinging to me, and I squirmed. Corbett said, "How are we going to cross that?"

"Fast," I said. "Don't breathe." I didn't move. I hadn't worked up the nerve.

"Come on, pals!" Billy hit the bridge at a dead run. As he went over the arch and disappeared from view, we heard him yell. The other side of the bridge would be steep. I hoped he'd rolled to the end and not over the edge. I wasn't ready to dive in after him, and I didn't hear anyone else volunteer.

"Billy?" I shouted. There was no answer.

"He's all right," Corbett said. His voice was hollowly reassuring. "Sure he is."

We looked at each other. We took deep breaths.

We scrambled up the arch, and when we could stand, we ran.

Was Billy down there? I made the mistake of looking from the top of the arch.

Down into a river of shit, chest-deep. A respectable crowd waded through it.

Disgust can freeze you as solid as fear. At my side, Corbett stopped to look where I was looking. He made a retching sound, took my arm and tried to pull me on. I couldn't move. I'd recognized someone I knew.

I called down. "George!"

Heads turned up. They were disguised by what was smeared across their faces, but that was George, all right. I tried to remember his last name and couldn't.

But he knew me. He shrank away with his sticky arms hiding his sticky head.

Benito had come back up the bridge. "Billy is safe." He spoke with the pinched voice of a man holding his breath. "Who was that?"

"An old friend. An advertising man, wrote fiction in his spare time. Not very good stories, but he wasn't a bad guy. How did he get here?"

"Immoderate flattery. There is no other way to reach this pit. Allen, Jerome, there is no profit in standing here. You cannot enjoy the view."

Immoderate flattery? It fit, in a way. Big Juju's way. Most advertising is immoderate praise of a product or its users. But like every other torture I'd seen in Hell, it was just too damned much! I wanted to tell George . . . what? That he'd been wronged? That I'd get justice for him no matter what it took? That I couldn't save him and I couldn't save myself and everything was useless because we were in the hands either of a cruel God or heartless aliens? I don't know. But I'd remembered one of his own ads, and I shouted it down to him. It was not to mock him! Only to get his attention!

"You *deserve* to belong to the Xanadu Country Club!"

The response was an explosion of voices. Smeared stinking heads rose, mocking voices called. "The wet-head is dead!" "Aren't you glad you use Dial? Don't you wish everybody did?" "I'm Glenda! Fly me!" "Hazel, it turned *blue!*" "Always have . . . *always* will!"

And we three who peered into the moat, we saw where the shit came from.

Another macabre joke. Every one of them had been fitted with a second anus. It became apparent only when they tried to speak.

Corbett bent double, heaving, a ghost trying to expel emptiness from the ghost of his belly. I tried to help him, but he backed away fast. He didn't want to be touched. The convulsions went on and on.

I tried to turn away from the edge, but it was too late. George screamed up at me, in agony. "Allen! Why?"

"I'm sorry!" I should have left him alone.

Benito spoke in an actor's voice, calm but carrying. "There is a way out of Hell."

He got insults and laughter, but a few listened.

"You must climb the pit. Cooperate if you must. It will be hard, but you can do it if you try long enough. Then you must move inward. The route to Heaven is at the center of Hell."

Smeared faces turned away. George stayed to answer. His laugh had tears in it. "Me, in Heaven? With shit dribbling down my chin? I'd rather stay here."

Another called. "Listen, when you get there, tell Him. Tell God we will praise Him day and night! I have written a new hymn to His name! Tell Him!"

Benito turned sadly away.

I looked for Corbett—and found him at the outer end of the bridge. He was crying and hiccoughing and trying to run. I shouted, "Corbett! Wrong way!"

He turned. "No chance! I don't belong here! I'm supposed to be in the winds!"

"You'll never get up the cliff."

"I will! Somehow, I will! I belong up there, not down here with—" He flapped his arms helplessly. Corbett had no word for these thoroughly damned souls with whom Corbett would not associate. He went away from us.

Billy was waiting at the inner end of the bridge. He watched us come down, then, "Where's Jerry?"

Benito shook his head. "Pride. He was too proud to stay."

PART III

20

THE THIRD GULLY WAS NARROWER AND CLEANER. From the edge it looked empty, so that I wondered if there were a sin nobody would commit, or one nobody thought of. But lights danced dimly down there . . .

From the arch it was clearer. I made out long rows of holes cut into the stone. The holes had raised stone rims. Most of them were occupied, each by a pair of human feet sticking straight up into the air. The feet danced. Flames burned on their soles.

"Another obsolete sin," said Benito. "Selling holy offices. Simony."

Billy said, "Huh?"

I translated for him. "Those guys would take money to make you a priest."

There were signs by some of the holes. "Wharton School of Theology. Earn your Th.D. in just ten weeks! Write Registrar for application."

And another: "Meditation. The new way to inner peace and serenity. Meet the greatest guru of all time. Registration fee, $350."

Billy was aghast. "God does *that* to them? Just for *that?*"

"They stole what belongs to God," Benito said. "There are popes in those baptismal fonts. And many others. The denomination does not seem important. What matters is the sale of the gifts of God."

Why would aliens care about that? Well, Carpentier?

"Benito, I don't like it here," Billy said.

I patted his shoulder. "Me neither. Let's get out." I felt the urge to run. At least I was safe from this pit. We all were. We'd never had heavenly gifts to sell.

The bridge over the fourth gully was just ahead, and I glanced into it from the top, intending to run on past. The strange sight held me. The damned flowed beneath us, and their heads had been turned back to front. Most of them were women.

"Fortune tellers," Benito said before I could ask. "They tried to see the future by magic."

And now they were not even allowed to watch where they were going. I shivered, thinking that a science-fiction writer might well end up here. But no, I'd never used magic. Only logic, and it hadn't kept me out of Hell. "Why aren't all the scientists and economic prognosticators here?" I asked. "*They* try to foresee the future."

"Most of these appealed to Satan for aid. He gave it to them . . . or not. It is the appeal that weighs against them." He turned to move on.

Then I recognized one of the damned.

A little elderly lady, very prim and proper. She'd been a teacher in my nephew's school. Now she walked with her head turned backward, and tears ran down her spine and between her buttocks. I screamed. The damned looked up at me.

"Mrs. Herrnstein! Why?" I shouted.

She looked away. Then she stopped and looked up. Face and back turned toward us. She'd always been thin, and I'd never thought of her as particularly feminine. Certainly she wasn't feminine now. "I belong here, Mr. Carpentier," she called. "Please leave. I don't want to be watched."

"You *belong* here?" I could *not* see Mrs. Herrnstein with a crystal ball.

"Yes. Whenever I had a pupil who had difficulty learning to read, I used—I was a bad teacher, Mr. Carpentier."

"You were a *good* teacher! You taught Hal more in a year than he learned in five!"

"I was a good teacher with good pupils. But I could not be bothered with the ones who weren't so bright. If they had trouble learning to read, I said they had dyslexia."

"Are you here because of bad diagnoses?" This was monstrous!

"Dyslexia is not a diagnosis, Mr. Carpentier. It is a prediction. It is a prediction that says that this child can never learn to read. And with that prediction on his record—why, strangely enough, none of them ever do. Unless they happen on a teacher who doesn't believe in educationese witchcraft."

"But—"

"It was witchcraft, Mr. Carpentier. Please go now." She walked on, crying uncontrollably, her face toward us as she walked away. I watched until she was out of sight.

"She does not belong here," I insisted.

"Then perhaps she will not be here long," Benito answered dispassionately. "Yet—you will note that she did not agree with your judgment."

"Then she's wrong too!"

"Why do you feel so competent to judge everyone, Allen?"

"Get it through your thick head that it's *Big Juju* I'm judging—"

"It is God you are judging," he thundered.

"All *right*, it's God I'm judging. If He can judge me, I claim the right to judge Him!"

Billy seemed horrified by what I was saying. I was sorry for that. But Benito laughed and said, "How will you implement your judgment against God Himself?"

The only possible answer to that was a feeble one, maybe, but I used it. "By withholding my worship. Benito, do you realize that the God you worship keeps a private torture chamber?"

"Hardly private."

"Private or public, the God Allen Carpentier worships will have to meet higher standards than *that!*"

Benito didn't speak for a moment. Then he said, "We must hope our shouting was not heard. Look ahead."

From our position at the top of the arch we had a good view of the rims of the next gully. On both sides of the gap, horned black demons moved. They were larger than men, a little smaller than the demons in the first ditch, but like them they had horns and tails, and their skin was black ebony, very different from a black man's skin. They carried—

"Pitchforks?"

"Certainly," said Benito.

I couldn't help grinning a little. Pitchforks! I'd forgotten that detail. Had Walt Disney's cartoonists ever realized why their devils carried pitchforks?

"They must not see us," Benito said. "None of us

are safe from them. They guard the pit of the grafters, of those who stole from positions of trust."

Billy shuddered. "Reckon they'd like me," he said. "Guess I took a few things from my bosses in my day. Not much, but some."

"Not me. Free-lance writers don't have bosses," I said. Then I remembered the advance from Omniverse Publishing, nine years before I died. Somehow the novel had never jelled, and *let's play it safe here, Carpentier. Demons wouldn't understand the publishing business.*

There was cover at the bottom of the bridge. It was all a jumble of boulders. We waited our chance, then sprinted down the bridge while none of the demons were nearby. We were hidden before another group came past. We huddled together between the rocks.

"Too bad the bridges are staggered," I whispered. "We could have gone right across." The next bridge was thirty or forty yards to the left, with a troop of twenty-odd demons between.

"For us this is the second most dangerous place in Hell," whispered Benito. "We must reach the next bridge without being seen. Cross at a dead run, and do not stop at the next pit. Run straight into it. There are no bridges in any case, and we could not reach one if any existed. The demons are on both sides of the pit."

Billy shifted restlessly. "Don't like running from nothing."

"We must," Benito said simply. He pointed. A demon strode past.

A roughly human form nine feet tall, equipped with horns and hooves and a twitching tail. A capriform humanoid.

How glib, Carpentier. Capriform humanoid? Demon! Why play games with yourself?

The demon was carrying a human being, carrying him like a bowling ball, his claws inserted deep into the man's back. The man writhed and struggled. The demon didn't seem to notice. He called to three of the others. "How many New Yorkers this week?"

They joined him in front of our rock. One twitched his tail up to his mouth. Teeth like butcher knives gnawed at the end. "Twelve."

"Make it thirteen. And it's still Thursday on Earth. If Hideous wins the pool again I'll rip his face off."

"You could forget to report this one."

"Why not?" The first demon lifted his human burden to study it. "He hardly counts anyway. He stole a few hundred bucks from a friend who needed an eye operation." He addressed the man: "*You* won't tell on us, will you?"

"No. I swear," said the man. His voice was choked with agony.

"And you won't show your head above the pitch? Because if we see any sign of you—" The demon hefted his pitchfork suggestively. "We'll pull you out and tear you in little pieces and scatter you widely. It hurts a *lot*."

"I won't tell," said the man.

"Good," said the demon holding him, and he flung him. The man dropped below the rim with a mournful howl that ended in a sound half splash, half thud.

"What's down there?" Billy whispered.

I answered, "Boiling pitch."

"What'd he do?"

"Graft."

"I kept wanting to try to save him."

Benito said, "I would not save him if I could."

The demons passed on. Like the warriors around the lake of blood, they looked always into the pit, always away from us. If we were careful we could move, one at a time, flitting from rock to rock to—

"Gotcha!" a demon shouted, and I had a heart attack, right out there between two inadequate boulders. All they had to do was come and collect me, but they weren't looking. They were clumped at the rim, jabbing down.

A human form came up dripping gobbets of black pitch and trying to wriggle free of the tines of two pitchforks. I heard, "Boss Tweed, ain't it? We been checking with some of those dead men that're supposed to have voted your ticket— Hold him, Crazyred!" The man lurched free of one pitchfork, but the other held him fast. They beached him. They began to play with him.

I touched Billy's shoulder. "Don't look. We can get a good way while they're busy."

We crawled like snakes. By the time the shade of Tweed had stopped screaming, we were opposite the bridge. I looked back once and had to close my eyes. The demons had opened him up and spread him out like a frog in biology class; but unlike the frog, he was still trying to get away.

Benito crouched like a sprinter. "Ready?"

"Yeah."

"Right."

We ran.

I heard a great bass roar of rage. I didn't look back. But as I went over the arch, last in line, I saw that the demons on the far side of the gully were running to meet us.

One was going to make it.

I stopped. Only for an instant; then I plunged down the arch behind Benito.

But Billy had doubled his speed.

The demon reached the end of the bridge off

balance and skidding. "Come to Poppa!" he roared, and swung his pitchfork around.

He was a nanosecond late. Billy shot past the tines and ran up the demon and swarmed over the huge head.

The demon bellowed and tried to reverse eighteen feet of iron pitchfork. Benito slammed shoulder-first into his knee. The demon half-turned, and I hit the other knee sideways. Both huge legs went out from under the demon, left him blind and falling.

Half a ton of demon slammed into the rock.

Billy rolled away. The demon moaned and tried to gather his knees to his chest.

"Now run!" cried Benito. *"Billy!"*

A troop of demons was almost on us. I raced for the next pit, stopped at the edge. Where was Billy?

Billy had retrieved the demon's pitchfork and was raising it for the kill.

I yelled, "Never mind that!" and then it was just too late. Billy yelled triumph and brought the pitchfork down hard. He raised it for another thrust, and they had him. I jumped into space alongside Benito. Three-inch fingernails clicked shut behind my neck.

21

THE SIDE OF THE GULLY WAS ROUGH ROCK FALLING almost sheer. I glimpsed it in free-fall, and when I saw that there were no handholds I simply gave up. A couple of seconds later I lay broken at the bottom, staring up at the non-sky.

In the sea of pain I couldn't tell what was broken and what was only bruised. But I remembered that you're not supposed to move an accident victim. I didn't try to move.

Rustling near me.

"Benito?"

"Over here."

"Are you hurt?"

"Yes."

"Me too."

"We are out of their path, I think. We need only wait to heal."

Whose path? I was afraid to turn my head, but I turned my eyes. I found myself looking up along the fluted robe of a life-sized golden statue. No information there.

I said, "What about Billy?"

"Poor Billy. His urge to violence betrayed him."

"Don't be so damned philosophical. We've got to get him out of their hands!"

"How?"

"Well . . . first we wait to heal, I guess. Where would they put him? In the pitch with the Tammany types?"

"Look up along the edge of the gully."

Something like an endless length of rope was falling in loops across the sky. It dropped very slowly, as if almost weightless. As it came near I saw that it was thicker than rope, and there was a tuft on the end . . . Where had I seen something like that recently?

Above our heads it hesitated, then descended like a blind worm. For seconds it was hidden behind the rock slope. Then it began to rise . . . and the end was coiled around something that moved. Billy.

"Minos," I said. "It's his tail."

"Yes."

Before we could move, Billy would be back on the island in the river of blood—or in the river itself; he'd left the island of his own free will. He was beyond our reach. I sighed and turned my eyes from the tiny struggling figure and the infinite sprawl of Minos' tail.

And the statue had moved.

It had gone past me about one yard. I turned my head, regardless of consequences. My neck wasn't broken. And there were two bare human feet beneath the hem of the golden robe. One moved a good six inches as I watched.

"Benito. There are men in those things."

"And women too," said Benito. "Religious hypocrites."

He stood up carefully, testing to see if anything had healed. Apparently it had. He tried to help me up, but pain yelped in my ribs. I sat down against the slope to wait some more.

Golden robes moved past like snails. There were men and women in those golden idols, but I saw only bare feet and shadowed faces within enormous hoods. One stopped, and turned with the same excruciating slowness that characterized his walk, and said, "Are you lost?"

Benito said we weren't. I asked, "Are you?"

"Why, no. I think this is my proper place." His accent was thick and hard to identify. "I have been here long enough to be convinced that God thinks so too."

"How long is that?"

"Over a thousand years have passed on Earth, I'm told."

"That's a little hard to swallow," I said. "The English language isn't that old."

"I know," said the priest. "We teach each other. I learned this language from one who came here recently, an Amie Semple MacPherson. There is little else to do as we wander this endless channel, and you may imagine that it is easier to teach each other than to search for some companion who speaks our own language."

"Why," I asked, "don't you stop and sit down?"

The tired gray eyes studied me from within the golden cowl. "I could fall on you. But it may be that you do not know what you say. If I stop this robe grows hot. It is too hot now. It grows hot slowly, and it grows cool slowly. Now, good-bye." He began to turn away.

Benito said, "We could walk along with you."

"That would please me." He finished his turn and took one lurching footstep.

I got up. The ruined ribs only twinged. "How heavy is that robe?" I asked.

"I never weighed it. They tell me it is gilded lead. Perhaps a ton?"

"What did you do?"

"Does it matter? I was young, I had not been a priest for many years. But the end of the thousand years since Christ was born were drawing to a close. People began to fear the end of the world. I urged them to give away their property. To the Church. We became very wealthy."

"You could have given it back, afterwards."

"We did not."

"Did all of you end up here? The whole order?"

"No. Some truly thought the world would end. Some believed a wealthy Church could serve souls better. But I never believed the Second Coming could be predicted, and I enjoyed the wealth. I—do you need to know more? It was a good thing to be in the Church in those days."

Benito tapped my shoulder and pointed. "There is our way out. The rubble from the bridge."

It had been a bridge, high and arching like those we'd crossed before. Now it was a sloping pile of shattered rock. I looked at it curiously, but it didn't seem different from any other rock I'd seen, and I could see that normal laws of material strength didn't hold down here. It wasn't a surprise.

"What happened to it?" I wondered. "Earthquake?"

"I am told that all Hell shook at the moment of Christ's death," said the ex-priest.

"So says Dante," Benito added. "Afterwards, He came to Hell and threw down the great gate in the wall of Dis."

"He must have been mad about something. I suppose being crucified could do that to you."

"I would be less flippant, Allen. Look around you." Before I could answer, Benito had started climbing the ruined bridge.

It was still a ridiculous picture. Christ was supposed to be gentle. Using a whip on the temple money-changers was one thing; behaving like a comic-book hero was something else. I tried to imagine the bleeding, wounded, near-naked figure ripping those tremendous iron gates from their hinges, while the halo flamed angrily about His Head—

Then gave it up and climbed up after Benito. I tested each foothold, but some of the slabs slid down anyway. Near the top the rockslide ended, and we climbed by fingerholds and toeholds. There it was that I had to repress a sudden, violent urge to giggle.

Benito wouldn't have appreciated it. But—no wonder Christ was so upset. Some clerk must have tried to hand Him Form D-345t839y-4583.

The seventh pit was enormous. I stood at the end of the bridge and marveled at the thin fairy-span arching across. Carbon steel wouldn't have taken the stress; yet it was made of stone without mortar, like the fallen bridge behind us. Another miracle, and so what?

We started across.

It was dark down there. What I could see had a vaguely reptilian flavor to it: constant slow slitherings, and sudden flurries of violent motion.

Benito pulled at my arm. "Why do you dawdle, Allen?"

"What's down there?"

"Thieves. Theft is the most profitable of sins, and

very popular. Tell me, Allen, do you expect to see anything that pleases you?"

He had me there. I didn't. But— "I'm a writer. I've got ten men's curiosity. What's the hurry? Are we in danger here?"

"I remind you that we are fugitives."

I stared in astonishment. "Geryon could have stopped us. Minos could have stopped us. They didn't."

"The demons behind us would have. Oh, very well, Allen. The real danger is at the next pit. We must cross that quickly."

"Okay." And I looked down again.

Reptilian, yeah. There were men and women down there . . . and lizards ranging in size from Chihuahua to Great Dane, and snakes whose range was even greater. I watched a tiny scarlet lizard leap from a crack in a rock to bite a man on the neck. The man burned like flash paper, dazzling me. When I looked again he was congealing from a cloud of smoke.

Benito was watching me, not them. Let him wait.

The land was strewn with rocks of all sizes. A stout gray-haired woman came toward us, running a tortuous path, her eyes fixed on her path. It didn't help. Somehow she stepped between two rocks and fell sprawling, yelling in despair. The python that had been following her caught up as she tried to run on the ruined foot. It climbed her leg and bit her on the navel.

Woman and snake, they lay immobile. They began to change.

"Allen—"

I made a shushing gesture. They were changing, the snake sprouting arms and legs and head hair, the woman melting into a smooth limbless shape. Presently there was nothing left of the woman.

The slender man who had been a snake stood up smiling. "Thanks, Gladys," he said, and walked away.

"He stole her shape," I said. "I'll be buggered. He stole her shape!"

"She will grow it back. In life she was probably a buyer of stolen goods, what do you call it? A fence."

"Yeah. Wow."·

"Are you ready?"

"Yeah." I turned and followed him. Wow. He stole her shape. How does a science-fiction writer explain that? A computer-drawn hologram. Could be. It was pretty dark down there. But I didn't believe it.

The bridge dipped. We climbed down. Benito turned left on the ledge between the seventh and eighth pits. Benito was clearly uneasy. Interesting things were happening in the darkness on my left, but I looked into the darkness on my right for the danger Benito expected.

It looked like a swarm of fireflies, or like a freeway seen from an airplane, or—

> This aye night, this aye night,
> Every night and all,
> Fire and sleet and candlelight,
> And Christ receive thy soul.

Sleet I'd found in the Circle of Gluttons, and fire on the desert. Here at last was the candlelight: huge candle flames moving in darkness.

From the next bridge it was no clearer. Benito kept trying to hurry me along. "You will not see anything here. Are you so fond of Hell that you would linger?"

Slender flames moved down there in the yellow-and-black murk . . . and stopped, and clustered beneath us. I said, "Who are they?"

"Dante calls this the Bolgia of the Evil Counselors."

"That doesn't tell me a lot. And I still don't know what you're afraid of."

A voice answered from below . . . a voice with little of the human in it. It thrummed like a harp. It was coming from the tip of one of the huge flames. "He is afraid of his own homecoming."

I looked at Benito. He nodded, not looking at me.

"Come down!" one of the flames called to Benito. It was eerily compelling, that thrumming voice. The tip of the flame wavered, turned to me. "Throw him down, you, if you're an American! That's Mussolini! Benito Mussolini!"

Jolted, I turned to Benito. He shrugged.

Mussolini?

Another voice thrummed from the pit. "You *are* American. I know your accent. Do you understand? That's Mussolini! Throw the bastard down here where he belongs!"

"Who are you?"

"Does it matter? I approved the firebombing of Dresden."

A British voice spoke from the flames. "And I led the mission. We may belong here, Yank, but so does that Eytie swine."

Benito was backing away. When I went toward him, he turned and ran. I caught him at the edge of the next pit and tripped him. He fell heavily to the ground, and I sat on him. He was no match for me. "Mussolini!" I shouted.

"I pulled you out of a jinn bottle!" he protested.

"And led me here, deeper into Hell! I knew it all along!" Mussolini. What better choice for the Devil's agent, to wander through Hell corrupting souls already half corrupted? Hitler was probably loose too. If we'd run across him I'd have guessed earlier. I remembered all my suspicions, and all the unexplained things that had happened on the trip down. No wonder he could give orders!

Well, I knew who he was now, and I knew where he belonged. We were at the edge of the ninth pit, but I took him by the heels and dragged him back to the eighth. He thrashed like a fish. He clutched at rocks and pulled a couple out of the ground, for all the good that did him.

The pit flamed beneath us with the crowd gathered to welcome Benito home.

I rolled him over the edge. He gave a low cry as he dropped. Before he struck bottom he burst into flame. His was very bright, brighter than most around him.

I turned and went on.

22

I WALKED UNTIL I HAD TO STOP, UNTIL THE GROUND dropped away at my feet. There I stood like a machine whose program has run out. After all, where would I go?

Now I was utterly alone, with nobody to tell me about the geography of Hell, or warn me of the dangers—

—or make me go deeper into horror after horror when all I wanted to do was stop. Mussolini. Benito Mussolini, Il Duce of Italy. He hadn't even tried to deny it.

What an idiot I'd been. Why hadn't I recognized him, with that massive square jaw and high forehead? I remembered reading about him in history books. Benito Mussolini had escaped from his castle-prison in a glider flown by Hitler's Commando, Skorzeny, one of the most romantic figures of that war. No wonder Benito could fly a glider!

Mussolini the fascist. He invented fascism! Killer and leader of killers, thug, ally of Adolf Hitler . . . back to the anonymous flame, Mussolini, evil genius behind the Italian king. Down you go, Benito, who poured me from a bottle.

I stood there a long time before I realized what I was seeing.

In the ninth pit the damned staggered and lurched, slipping in bloody mud, leaving more blood to make the path more slippery for those behind. They seemed dazed survivors of some lost battle.

One showed no obvious wounds, except for his erect posture and painfully stiff walk. I stared at his face, where a macabre joke had been played. It was pale and lean, and calm; no one would have guessed that he was in pain; but the eyes burned with hate. The mustache was in an unfamiliar style, straight, but twice the width of his mouth. And the sharp white canine teeth protruding over his lower lip would have had anyone over the age of six shouting, "Vampire!"

Well ahead of him was a sturdy fat man with a striking bearded face and blood running from a cut throat. The face was familiar. I studied him, trying to remember where I'd seen that face.

He stared back. Then he roared in fury wrapped in a Shakespearean accent. "Varlet! Who might you be, that stare so arrogantly at England?"

"Huh?" I shook myself. "Carp— Carpenter."

"Come down, woodworker, and I will have your eyes nailed shut!"

I realized I had been staring, rudely, at people who had trouble enough without that. More of Big Juju's victims. "Sorry. Does it help if I tell you the wounds will heal?"

I could see the shock rippling down the line, and suddenly they were all screaming curses and waving their fists. One man threatened with his severed arm held like a club.

"Dolt! Ass who mocks us!"

"What did I say?"

"You cannot be such a fool!" "England" cried. "We are nearly healed now! We reach the point in the circle where—" He stopped, looking ahead, forgetting me entirely. "I see him now," he said in a voice without life or hope.

I looked. The bridge was ahead of them, and under it was a king-sized version of all the other demons we'd passed, twenty feet tall, carrying a slender sword. He grinned, showing teeth nearly a foot long.

I had to cross the bridge anyway. I walked toward the demon.

He was killing them. They marched toward him, hanging back when they could until others pushed ahead, and he killed them. He picked a man up and sliced him from the crotch to the throat, set him down and let him walk on. Empathic pain lashed through me, and a line from a joke ran crazily through my head. About a cowboy who'd been thrown onto a barbed wire fence. He'd shown Texas courage; he'd remounted the horse and gone on. *Of course he had to let the stirrups out a little . . .*

The fat man looked sick and scared. His face clicked suddenly into place: a painting, very famous. Henry the Eighth.

I kept walking.

I was crossing the bridge when Henry reached the demon. The sword was not a sword, I saw now. It was an overdeveloped fingernail on an overdeveloped middle finger as thick as a strong man's thigh. It flicked like a rapier and severed Henry's head, and the demon handed Henry his head, and Henry walked on. The sharp horn tip of the sword flicked suddenly up before my face.

I stopped.

"Who may you be, O privileged one, who run so free through Hell?"

I got my throat working. "Allen Carpenter."

"Where away, Carpenter?"

"I don't know. Inward." With all the feelings that had been burnt out of me, one was left. Curiosity. Whatever Benito had planned for me, it lay downward, inward.

The dead had stopped to wait, with understandable patience, for the demon to finish his conversation. I waved downward. "Who are they?"

The demon seemed in no hurry. "Sowers of discord. People who advocated hatred, started wars, refused to end wars—you know, the opposite of the peacemakers. This is a special collection. Religious schizmatics. Generally founded their own churches for their own purposes. You want political types, or lawyers who talked people into divorces they didn't want and lawsuits they didn't need, you've got to go to another part of the pit."

"Oh."

The demon looked fondly at "England's" receding back. "Henry there wanted a divorce. The Church wouldn't give him one. So he made himself a Church that would. Clever?"

"On the evidence, not very."

The demon stooped to pick up the man with the Fu Manchu mustache and the vampire teeth. "Dracula here didn't found any churches. He—"

"*Dracula!* I thought he was— Dammit, he *was* just a legend."

"There *are* legends about him. In his homeland, Transylvania, mothers still frighten their children with his name. Dracula was just a title. Means dragon. His real name was Vlad; they called him Vlad Tepes, Vlad the Impaler. He spent his whole life torturing

and killing Turks in the name of Christ. Otherwise
he'd be uphill, eyelash deep in boiling blood. About
half the people he killed were his own subjects, by the
way."

Small wonder Vlad the Impaler walked funny. A
wooden stake was sticking two feet out of his anus.
The demon didn't need his sword. He just pushed
the stake up until it didn't show, set the man down,
and let him walk on. Walking funny.

The demon picked up another. "Johann here was the
only man God would reveal the exact time of Dooms-
day to. He could save a small party of the Chosen,
chosen by him, that is. All you had to do was turn
all your property over to him." The demon grinned
enormously. "And you, Carpenter? Did you ever create
a church of your very own?"

"I—" Oh, boy.

The sword's bloody tip swung away and back,
rapier-quick. I ducked and ran. I fell flat on the bridge
as the sword flashed again. The demon couldn't quite
get at me at that angle. But the arch of the bridge
dipped low, there at the end.

I rose to sprint position, poised, took off. At the base
of the arch the sword flicked toward me at knee height.
I jumped it and kept running, right across and into
the space above the next pit.

The side was steep. I hit once, and bounced, and
hit the bottom very hard.

There was no unconsciousness in Hell. There was
only pain and the awful strain of trying to draw a
breath. Deep down behind the pain a tiny voice was
saying, *You don't need to breathe, Carpentier. You're
dead.* But I wanted to breathe, I needed to breathe,
and not a sip of air could I draw.

Eventually the air did come, in sips, then gulps. I

tried to straighten out. It felt as if I were breaking my own back. Maybe my back *was* broken. But the sword would have been worse.

Could I feel my feet? Yes.

Okay. Your spine's intact. Just lie here awhile. It will heal. Sure, we always healed.

Hey, Carpentier. Why was it Benito always healed before you did?

Why shouldn't he? He was one of the paid staff.

Then why did he get hurt at all?

A woman's voice said, "What've you got?"

"Uh?" I still couldn't get more coherent than that.

"What've you got?" she repeated patiently. I moved my head around, slowly. It was dark and gloomy. I became aware of hideous screeching sounds, moans, screams of pain and rage, snarling dogs, the cacaphony of Hell.

She was sitting against the sloping side of the trench, naked, her body marked with pustules and the scars of older eruptions of the skin. She didn't seem more able to move than I was.

But the pain in my back was easing. I said, "Broken back, probably. What've *you* got?"

"Everything. Syphilis. Gonorrhea. Yaws. Trench mouth. Everything you can think of."

"Uh huh. I know what *you've* been doing."

She wailed, "But I *didn't!* That's why it's so unfair!"

My eyes were getting accustomed to the gloom that hung thick down here in the pit. There were others lying about the floor and the sides of the gully. Most of them looked deathly ill.

Across from me was a man scrabbling among thousands of pills. There must have been every variety of medication ever invented or imagined: tablets, capsules of many hues, bottles of liquids, tiny pills and pills that would choke a horse. He groaned in pain as he held up a pill and squinted at it. Finally he decided: he flung the pill back into the bathtub of them next to him.

He sat for a moment. Then he moaned, pressing his hands hard against his belly. "It's eating me alive!" he screamed. He scrabbled for another pill. This time he gulped it without looking at it. It didn't seem to help, because he screamed even louder and went back to his inspection routine.

I looked a question at the girl. She shrugged. "He sold cancer cures. They only worked if you didn't go to a doctor. Somewhere in that pile there may be a pill that cures him."

"What about the rest?"

"Some don't do anything. Some make it worse."

I shuddered, then froze as something came howling past on all fours, foam dripping from its jaws. I'd thought it was an animal, but it wasn't. It was a man.

"Counterfeiters. Counterfeiters always get rabies," said the woman. "If they bite you it takes a long time to heal."

And I couldn't move! There was nothing to do but watch.

Men and women with peeling scabs and an itch that drove them to tear at themselves. A man with no ears, unable to move and screaming for water.

"Listen!" he shouted. "Tell Satan! Anyone! Tell Satan there is a plot to overthrow him. For water I will reveal the names of the plotters! Tell him!"

They were all deathly ill, and they were all in pain—

—except one, and he was startling by contrast. He sat against the slope of the gully, a few feet from the girl and across from me. A middle-aged cherub, comfortably overweight, his blue eyes twinkling above a mad and happy smile.

Certainly he was mad. Was it a sickness of the mind, or had some vile bacterium reached his brain?

I had to get out of here. The most ferocious contagious diseases ever to wrack mankind were all around me. I tried to move, and stopped at once. My legs wouldn't obey, and it felt as if my spine were being twisted in a vise. Had I caught something already? Spinal meningitis, maybe?

The madman's wandering blue eyes found me. He said, "I was a psychiatrist."

"I didn't ask." In fact, I'd already learned more of Hell than I really wanted to know. I only wanted out. *Don't tell me any more!* I closed my eyes.

"They trusted me," the mad voice said happily. "They thought we knew what we were doing. For fifty bucks an hour I listened to their life stories. Wouldn't you?"

He subsided. The woman said, "He's crazy."

"Thanks. I really wondered about that," I told her without opening my eyes.

"Listen, you fell in over the edge. Have you been upslope? Have you seen a lot of what's up there?"

"A lot."

"What do they do to, shall we say, ladies of the evening?"

I opened my eyes. She was tense, waiting for my words.

"I didn't notice anything special for whores. Why?"

"I, I . . . Listen, some girls don't actually sleep with the customers. They take a gentleman to a motel, they get their money in advance, then they disappear. Sometimes you can do better than that. You're just getting down to business when your boyfriend walks in the door. You see?"

"Sure." I'd been robbed that way a couple of times in England.

"Well," she said, "you'd think that wouldn't be as bad as being an actual . . . prostitute." And she looked at me.

Somehow the memory was very dim now, of a time on Earth when a London girl had propositioned me, taken my money, and vanished from a bathroom with an unsuspected second door, leaving me in rage and frustrated lust. If I'd caught her I'd have killed her. But that was long ago, and nothing looked bad next to where I was now.

So I lied. "They'd be downslope from here. I haven't been there yet."

Satisfied, she sank back and forgot me in the examination of her ruined body.

The mad psychiatrist noticed me again. "We were just playing," he said dreamily. "Tinkering with something we didn't understand. I knew. Oh, I knew. Let me tell you—"

"Don't tell me." They kept hurting at me, all of them!

"He was a catatonic. He was like a rubber doll. You could put him in any position, and he'd stay there for hours. We tried all sorts of things in those days. Shock therapy, insulin shock, lobotomy. Punish the patient for not noticing the outside world."

"Or for not noticing you."

I meant it to hurt, but he nodded happily. "So we put him in a hotbox and started raising the temperature. We watched him through a window. First he just sweated. Then he started to move around. At a hundred and thirty he said his first words in sixteen years. *'Get me the fuck out of here!'*"

The mad eyes found me, and his face seemed to cave in. The cherubic smile vanished. Urgently he said, "Get me the fuck out of here!"

"I can't. I'll be lucky to get out myself." I tried

moving again. There was pain, but not enough to keep me in that place. I stood gingerly and started up the slope.

The girl cried, "You can't do that! Come back here! Come back!"

I kept going. There were rocks to pull myself up, cracks to use as footholds. I'd climbed just far enough when another hydrophobia case raged past, biting and chewing on everyone he passed. A rock rolled from beneath my foot, and pain grated in my spine as I caught myself.

The rabid man screamed at the psychiatrist, but the cherubic look had returned and he was smiling dreamily at the opposite wall. When I reached the top I remembered who had been in the last pit of the Eighth Circle. Frauds. Falsifiers. False witnesses.

23

THE WAS THE LAST OF THE BOLGIAS. NOW THE WAY led across an empty, rocky land. I turned and looked at the ten canyons rising upward behind me, light flickering from some, others marked by rising smoke or roiling heated air. It had not been a pleasant journey.

Far ahead, through a twilit gloom that would just have had drivers turning on their headlights, I saw what seemed a cluster of great towers. There was nothing else to see, nothing at all.

Benito's evil counsel had brought me this far. Now it was too late. I could get back a little way, probably to the fifth pit, possibly as far as the cliff. But I'd never talk Geryon into taking me up that cliff . . . and there were just too many places where Allen Carpentier might belong.

Could I talk the monster into summoning Minos? That could get me all the way back to the Vestibule. Yeah, and into the bottle again. If I were lucky. I hadn't forgotten that burrowing this far into Hell might be a crime in itself. Minos had told me that I could choose far worse for myself than "justice." Maybe I'd already made the choice.

Or . . . I could just sit down. In this empty borderland I could spend a good piece of eternity before some angel noticed me.

I sat down.

It was very peaceful.

It was, in fact, the only completely empty spot I'd seen in Hell. Why? Maybe it was reserved for some brand new sin, something that hadn't been invented yet . . . say, a development of brain research or genetics. At some time in the indefinite future I might have to vacate fast.

Meanwhile, it was better than the bottle. I could see my navel.

Time passed without leaving footprints. Days, I think. The stinks of Hell were still in my nostrils. The ever-present background noise might have been soothing if I hadn't known what it was: millions of moans and cries blended by distance. But nobody was hurting me or hurting at me. I didn't have to watch people getting sliced up, or burned, or riddled by diseases, or smashed by demon cars, or distorted into obscene shapes.

I sat and dreamed of the past. I wondered idly about the looming towers I could see in the dark distance. I wondered at Benito's ultimate purpose in luring me here. But none of it seemed to matter. I thought that even curiosity had been burned out of me.

That would have been nice. I would have liked to turn my mind off for a long time. But it wouldn't turn off. Whatever quiet I'd found here, there was still Hell around me, and I hurt with the need to know why.

God had created human souls; could He not uncreate the failures? God had created sleep; could He not put the failures to sleep, forever? There were no good excuses for Hell. I thought of some unsettling bad ones:

The universe would fly off its axis if Hell's agony did not balance Heaven's bliss.

Or: Part of Heaven's bliss was the knowledge that lots of nasty people were suffering terribly.

Or the old standby: We were in the hands of infinite power and infinite sadism.

I got restless. The towers kept catching at my eye: blurred gray shadows on the horizon. Skyscrapers? A city in Hell? Quarters to house the maintenance crew for Infernoland? Or were they the true entrance, the tourist entrance?

But I was only playing with plots. I didn't believe in Infernoland anymore. This was Hell, and I knew it. I finally realized what was really bothering me.

To all intents and purposes I was back in the bottle.

I got up. I walked toward the towers. No harm in looking.

They weren't towers.

They were giants, enormous humanoids, buried in the earth from the navel down. I stopped well out of their reach to study them. Their enormous eyes found me and pinned me to the landscape like a butterfly on a board, then shifted away. I was not worth their attention.

I was glad. Unreasonably I felt that those tremendous deep eyes could see everything there was to know about me.

One was mad. He looked down at me hopefully and said, "Ildurb fistenant imb?" His face fell when I did not respond. Alien language, alien being. What were these aliens doing in human Hell?

Not serving Big Juju. Not hardly. Miles of chain bound their arms to their sides.

There were giants in the Bible and Titans in mythology. But no archaeologist had ever found human bones this size. And how could they survive Earth's gravity? The square-cube law should have flattened them into mountains of hamburger.

Maybe they weren't from this universe at all. An attacking army from another universe made by another creator? The science-fiction writer in me, the late Allen Carpentier, wanted very much to see their legs and feet. They must be disproportionately large and sturdy to support their weight . . . unless they had developed in a lighter gravity field . . .

While Carpentier the trapped damned soul was examining the chains that wrapped another of the giants.

For the giants were buried just outside a chin-high wall: their chins, not mine. The wall looked too smooth to climb. I walked up to the chained giant, ready to jump, but it wasn't necessary. The chain looked like anchor cable. Whoever had wrapped it round him had a fine eye for detail. He'd have been lucky to shrug his eyebrows.

Now, what would Benito have done here? Climbed the giant, of course.

The thought of climbing such a monster gave me pause. Yet I was sure I could do it. Up the chain, stepping in the links, as far as his shoulder; beware of snapping teeth. Then onto the wall and down.

If Benito had told the truth . . . if what I remembered of Dante was true . . . I would then be in the last Circle of Hell, the Circle of Traitors. Traitors to nation, to overlord, to benefactor, to parents and siblings. A great ice plain, and the traitors embedded in it. There would be nothing but the cold to stop me from crossing it, and I knew I couldn't freeze to death.

It looked so easy. What had Benito left out?

I remembered the great ice plain well enough. The college boy had been jolted at finding part of Hell already frozen over. Benito hadn't said anything that jarred with my own memories of Dante.

But there had to be a joker in the deck somewhere. Benito had been a power in Hell. He'd given orders to others of Hell's minions. He'd demonstrated demonic strength against a tank of a man in the great swamp.

Carpentier, why didn't he do that to you?

Maybe it was guilt that stopped him. He'd writhed and torn at the ground, but he hadn't actually hit me, not once. He'd uprooted jagged rocks while trying to use them as anchors, but he hadn't tried to hit me with them. And for all his presumed safe-conduct, he was back where Minos had sentenced him, with the Evil Counselors.

Maybe Satan or God or Big Juju had rendered some kind of judgment against Benito. With me as the agent.

But *why hadn't Benito fought?*

The giant tried to shake himself. The chains barely rustled.

No danger there.

You writhe and you struggle, but there's no way around it. Me too, giant. From every possible direction it looked the same. It was going to be unreasonably easy for Allen Carpentier to enter the Circle of Traitors . . . the place of punishment for those who had betrayed their benefactors.

I thought it over for a long time. Then I turned and started back.

24

GOING BACK WAS HARDER. THE DIP AT THE LOWER END
of the tenth bridge was steeper, and now I was climbing it. I crossed the pit without looking down and
climbed backward down the high end of the bridge.

I saw the next bridge close by, and made for it.

A sword's point flicked up before my eyes. I
stopped. Surely he'd been under a different bridge? I'd
skewed my path deliberately. But a half-human, half-
bestial head beyond the sword's point shook itself
negatively.

"You can't go back, Carpenter."

"I have to."

The blade hung before me, rock-steady. I could
have chinned myself on it. I half-stepped forward and
the blade moved too fast to follow. Now it pricked
the tip of my nose.

I shrugged and turned back.

I took no chances. I crossed the inner pit again and
circled through the wasteland beyond. Two bridges
away, I crossed again—on my belly. I slid down the
high end of the bridge and kept crawling along the

ridge above the ninth pit. He couldn't be under *all* the bridges.

Couldn't he just. Like the damned clerk. He was waiting when I tried to stand up. At this, the low side of the pit, he had the angle on me. "You can't go up-hill," he said. "I really don't know how to make it plainer."

"I'm from the Vestibule," I said. "I don't belong here."

"You never created your own Church, Carpenter?"

Oh, dammit! "Listen, those weren't in competition with God or anybody! All I did was make up some religions for aliens. If that was enough you'd have every science-fiction writer who ever lived!"

"We've got *him*," said the demon, and he pointed with the sword.

I forgot the sword entirely. I leaned far out over the edge of the pit to see. "What in Hell—to coin a phrase—is that?"

It was, in a sense, the last word in centaurs. At one end was most of what I took for a trilobite. The head of the trilobite was a gristly primitive fish. Its head was the torso of a bony fish . . . and so on up the line, lungfish, proto–rat, bigger rat, a large smooth-skinned beast I didn't recognize, a thing like a gorilla, a thing like a man, finally a true man. None of the beasts had full hindquarters except the trilobite; none had a head except the man. The whole thing crawled along on flopping fish-torsos and forelegs and hands, a tremen-dous unmatched centipede. The human face seemed quite mad.

"He founded a religion that masks as a form of lay psychiatry. Members try to recall previous lives in their presumed animal ancestry. They also recall their own past lives . . . and that adds an interesting blackmail angle, because those who hear confession are often more dedicated than honorable. Excuse me."

For the line of victims had bunched up while we talked. The demon turned and sliced at them rapidly, to a tune of screams and curses. The centaur creature he sliced into its separate components, and it went past him in a parade, on arms and forelegs and wriggling fishy fins. The sword flicked up again just as I'd decided to make a break for it.

A bead of blood formed at the tip of my nose. "I'm not like him," I said quickly. "He played the game for real. With me it was just a game." I backed away until the tenth *bolgia* was an emptiness beneath my heels. He couldn't reach me now. "Take the Silpies. They were humanoid but telepaths. They believed they had one collective soul, and they could prove it! And the Sloots were slugs with tool-using tentacles developed from their tongues. To them, God was a Sloot with no tongue. He didn't need a tongue; He didn't eat, and He could create at will, by the power of His mind." I saw him nodding and was encouraged. "None of this was more than playing with ideas."

The demon was still nodding. "Games played with the concept of religion. Enough such games and all religions might look equally silly."

"You can't do this!" I shouted. "Listen, there's a friend of mine in the Eighth Bolgia, and it's my fault he's there, and I've got to get him out!"

"Did anyone promise you it would be easy? Or even possible?"

"Whatever it takes," I said, and thought I meant it.

"Step closer."

I walked to the edge. Carpentier shows his good faith.

The sword flashed twice. I heard and felt the tip grate along my ribs. It left two vertical slashes along my chest and belly. I reeled back with my arms wrapped around myself to hold my guts in.

The demon was watching me steadily. What could he be waiting for?

I knew. I stepped forward and dropped my arms. Carpentier shows his inability to learn.

The sword flashed twice more, leaving two deep horizontal slashes, perhaps mortally deep. A living man would have fainted from shock. I couldn't.

"Games," said the big evil humanoid. "Your move."

I studied the slashes and the flowing blood. Shock did seem to be slowing down my thought processes, but presently I saw what he meant. I said, "What do I use for a pencil?"

"You'll think of something."

I studied my fingernails. I thought of something.

I gouged a ragged X in the top left square of the diagram. The sword flashed to place an O in an adjacent corner.

I climbed the first slope of the bridge on fingers and toes. When I could walk I held my arms wrapped around myself, holding me in. The pride of my victory seemed excessive for a stupid game of ticktacktoe.

As I left the bridge I heard him call, "Carpenter?"

I turned my head.

"Best two out of three?"

My imagination was dead of shock. The only dirty word I could think of was one I'd never use again, not after seeing the place of the flatterers. I just kept walking along the rim.

The eighth pit was a canyon filled with firelight. "Benito!" My voice echoed hollowly between the canyon walls. "Benito!"

Some of the flames wavered. Thrumming voices,

retarded by the transfer from voice to flame tip, floated upward.

"Leave the damned to suffer alone."

"Benito who?"

"Bug off, you!"

The canyon stretched endlessly away in both directions in a gentle curve. If it was a full circle, it could hold millions. How was I to find Benito?

"Benito!" There was panic in my voice. The strain hurt my slashed chest. "Benito!"

"Benito Mussolini? He just passed me going *that* way—"

"No, it was the other direction."

"You're both wrong. Mussolini's in the boiling lake."

A fat lot of help I'd get here. And if I found him, what then? How was I going to get him out?

How did he get out in the first place? Maybe he'd already left again. A frustrating thought, because I couldn't do a thing about it, and it would mean I'd played my game with the demon for nothing. I hoped Benito was already out, but I had to assume he was still in there.

The canyon wasn't all that deep. What I needed was a climber's rope. Yeah, an asbestos one, stupid! Benito was on fire! For that matter, I hadn't seen any ropes anywhere.

I thought for a second about the chain on the giant. It would mean passing the demon twice—

No. Even if I got the chain loose, it was too heavy to move, and the freed giant would probably crush me for my trouble. I was glad I didn't have to decide to face the demon's sword again. I don't know what I would have done.

Well? *Think, Carpentier! There are tools in Hell. Sure, boats carry rope. Now we're getting somewhere. A heavy rope, kept wet while Benito climbs— Wait a minute. How do we climb the cliff when there's no rope yet? There haven't been any boats since the gaudy alien Geryon took us down. Tackle Geryon again?*

And if it doesn't work, back in the bottle while Benito burns?

Benito was smarter than I was. Maybe he'd think of something. "Benito!"

Mocking, thrumming voices answered.

I thought of fourteen feet of sword blade attached to a twenty-foot demon. Disable the demon (with what?), cut the blade loose (how?), send it down to Benito. But could he climb something that sharp? Or would he lose his fingers immediately? Did fingernail burn?

Waitaminute! There were smaller demons, higher up, carrying iron pitchforks!

I made for the bridge. In a few steps I was running. If I slowed down I'd want to stop, because I was terrified of what I planned.

I was in too much of a hurry. I was trotting toward the base of the tremendous bridge over the chasm of thieves when something flashed scarlet from behind a rock. I turned, frowning . . .

. . . and there was agony, flashing out from my neck to engulf me and drown me. I felt my bones soften and bend.

The pain drew back like a broken wave receding, but it left a blackened mind. I was confused; I couldn't think. A homely bearded man bent over me, saying urgent words that made no sense.

"Which way is out?" He was huge, I realized. A giant. I stepped toward him—and I was tiny and four-legged; my belly scraped the ground. A lizard. I was a lizard.

The bearded man repeated himself, enunciating each word. "Which way is out? How can I leave Hell?"

Vengeance. I advanced on him. Bite the son of a bitch! He backed away, still talking, but I couldn't understand him.

He stopped and seemed to brace himself.

I leapt. I sank my teeth into his belly. He howled, and I dropped to the ground, writhing in new agony.

When my mind cleared I was a man. I rolled away fast from the red lizard and didn't stop until there was a rock between us. The lizard stayed where he was, watching me.

I was making for the next bridge when his words came back to me. My dumb reptile brain had registered them only as sounds.

"You can't speak!" he'd wailed. Then, "Tell me! I'll let you bite me, but tell me the way out!"

He was a scarlet splash on a gray rock. Still watching me.

I pointed downslope, toward the lake of ice. "There! All the way to the center, if I haven't been lied to myself!"

I glanced back once after I'd crossed the next bridge. The lizard was poised on the rim, staring down. As I watched, he made his decision. He leapt into the pit.

Now what was that all about? *Never mind, Carpentier, you've got other concerns . . .*

25

Far below me, the golden monks stood like so many statues. Every couple of seconds one or another would rock forward as if its base were unstable. The broken bridge dropped in a cascade of rock.

I stopped to catch my breath (Habit, Carpentier! You could give that up), then went down the broken slope with some care. It would have been easy to break an ankle.

I had reached the floor of the canyon before I noticed that one of the monks had turned completely around to stare at me. His slate-gray eyes were the oldest, the weariest I had ever seen, and I recognized them.

He said, "Didn't you pass here a week ago?"

"A few days, I think. And you've only come this far?"

"We hurry as fast as we can." The gray eyes studied me. They were so tired; they made me want to sag down and rest. "May I ask, what game are you playing? Are you a courier or something equally unlikely?"

"No. I—" Why not tell the truth? He wasn't about

to run tell someone. "I've got to steal a pitchfork from one of the ten-foot demons in the next pit over."

"Don a cloak like mine," he said. "See what it does to your sense of humor."

I sank down against the bank. Those tired eyes . . . "I'll wear the cloak," I said. "You get Benito out of the Pit of the Evil Counselors. Okay?"

"I beg your pardon?"

"I pushed a good friend into the Pit of the Evil Counselors. If I can't—"

"But why would you do a thing like that?"

I howled. It startled me more than him. I'd been about to say something else entirely. But no words came, and I threw back my head and howled. The tears streamed down my face.

The monk said something in a foreign language. He tottered toward me and stopped. He didn't know what to do. "There, there," he said. "It will be all right. Don't cry." With a touch of bitterness he added, "Everyone will notice."

There was a howl as big as the world inside me. It wanted out, and it was stronger than I was. I howled.

The priest muttered to himself. Aloud he said, "Please. Please don't do that. If you will only stop crying, I will help you get your pitchfork."

I shook my head. I got out a whimpered, "How?"

He sighed. "I cannot even take off my robe. I do not see how I can help. Perhaps I could act as bait somehow?" He lifted his head, his teeth grinding with the effort, to look up along the cascade of broken rock.

I stood up. I patted him on his leaden back: *Clunk, clunk, clunk.* "You've got your own problems." I girded up my mental loins and started up the slope.

Loose rocks rolled under my feet. This was the high side of the gully. It took a long time to get to the top. I had just one advantage: part of the bridge still projected out from the cliff. I climbed in its shadow and stopped underneath. I waited.

After all, what could a demon do to me? Rip me to pieces? I'd heal.

Drop me into the pitch forever?

Throw me into the Pit of the Thieves?

One of the horned black demons strolled past, his head turned to study the pitch on the other side of the ridge. He held six yards of iron pitchfork balanced in one hand. All I had to do was leap out and grab it.

I let him go. When he was past I began to shake. The beast had three-inch claws, ten. And eight-inch tusks, two. And Carpentier was a coward.

I heard clanking and puffing below me. I turned and saw an amazing sight. The priest was coming up behind me.

I watched him. I didn't believe it, but it was true: he was actually in motion. He sounded as if he were dying again, but every so often his hand or his foot would move and he'd be two inches higher. When I finally made myself believe what was happening, I scrambled down the cliff, got under him and pushed up on the rigid hem of his robe. I doubt it helped. I might as well have been trying to lift the world.

We reached a flattish fragment of rock just under what was left of the bridge. There we rested. The death rattle was in his throat. His eyes were closed. His face glistened.

"Thousand years," he got out. "Been walking . . . thousand years . . . in this lead coffin. Legs like trees." Then, "Was a priest. A priest. Supposed to . . . keep people *out* of Hell."

"I still don't know how we're going to do it." The *we* was courtesy, and he deserved it. But what could he do?

"Get me up," he said.

I got my arms under his robe. It was warm. Together we got him upright, somehow. Then I looked
up . . . at a demon's hooves.

The demon looked down at us, grinning. "You
know," he said pleasantly, "you're the first one ever
got this far out of the tar."

I said, "You're making a mistake. I'm not—" Then
I leapt for it. The pitchfork struck sparks from the
rock where I'd been, but I was in midair, falling.

I landed hard on a ragged-edged boulder. I rolled
immediately, ready to dodge again.

The priest was gripping the business end of the
pitchfork!

The demon bellowed and pulled. For an instant he
had lifted the priest off the rock, robe and all. Then
the priest sagged back, still gripping the tines.

I tried to climb up to help.

The priest took two steps back and off the edge of
the rock.

The demon bellowed for help. He was trying to lift
half a ton of leaden robe, and it wasn't working out.
I had almost reached them when the demon cried out
and let go. The priest dropped through space.

I crawled down to him.

The robe was bent like tinsel and cracked down
the front. The edges glowed yellow. He'd been told
wrong; the robe was solid gold. When I touched it it
burned my fingers.

The priest was mangled inside. He looked violently
dead, except for his eyes, which followed me. If I
didn't get him out of the robe he'd fry. But you don't
move an accident victim—

He'll heal, Carpentier. We all heal, to be hurt again.
I pulled him out by his feet. The robe wasn't con-
toured to let him pass, but it didn't matter. He came

out like a jellyfish. He must have broken every bone in his body.

I spoke, not to the soft-looking head but to the gray eyes alone. "You'll heal. When you heal, there's a way out of Hell. Benito says so. Go downhill. Downhill."

The eyes blinked.

"I've got to rescue Benito," I said. I pulled him over to the side so nobody would step on him. I picked up the pitchfork and left.

"Benito!"

I walked the ridge between the pits, calling like a lost soul. The answering voices all sounded the same, anonymous, thrumming, inhuman. "Here I am, fellah!" "Benito who?" "Who dares disturb the silence of Hell?"

"Benito!"

"Allen?"

That had to be him! But a dozen voices took it up. "Allen!" "Here I am, Allen! What kept you?"

"Benito! I've come to get you out!"

I listened for the Italian accent . . . and heard it. "Never mind. I belong here. I should not have tried to leave."

All the flames looked alike, but I thought I had him placed now. I reached down with the pitchfork. "Bugger that! Grab the end!"

The other flames were wandering off. Benito said, "It is not long enough in any case."

It wasn't. I looked along the rim. There was a rough place where I might climb down partway.

Benito tried to stop me. "You are being stupid. If you fall, you will burn like the rest of us!"

"Can you reach the end?"

"Go away, Allen. This is my proper place."

I was ten feet below the rim and almost out of footholds. The pitchfork was heavy and awkward. I tried to go further, setting my feet very carefully.

"All right," Benito said suddenly. The huge flame moved to engulf the tines. I felt a feather touch on the haft, and the flame began to rise from the pit.

He called, "Can you hold me?"

I laughed wih relief. "You don't weigh as much as an ounce! I could lift a thousand of you!" After all I'd been through, suddenly it was going to be easy.

The flame rose higher along the haft . . . and I felt the first warming of the metal.

I waited until I was sure I could filter the panic from my voice. Some of it may have got through anyway. "Benito? Hurry."

"Is something wrong?"

"No, never mind. Just hurry." I was afraid he'd let go.

The metal was uncomfortably warm.

It grew hot.

Down there where a huge flame was rising in dreamy sloth, the metal began to glow dull red. He wouldn't notice; his own bright flame would blind him to it. Up here it was too hot to hold, but I held on, my teeth clenched against the scream.

The scream grew bulky in my throat. I stopped breathing to hold it in. If Benito gave up now to save me pain, I'd never, never find the courage to do this twice.

The metal was cherry red around the flame. My hands began to sizzle. I wasn't breathing, but the smell of cooked meat worked its way into my nose. I couldn't imagine how my hands still held. I was clenching them with everything I had, but the muscles and nerves must be cooked through. Charred through. I knew that smell too: dinner ruined. My head was

thrown back, my eyes clenched tight. There was no
sensation but the fire.

"You can let go," said Benito. He was beside me,
clinging to the cliff, his body no longer hidden by the
flame.

I tried to let go.

My hands were charred fast to the haft. I tried to
knock the pitchfork loose. It came loose, all right, and
slid bumping into the eighth *bolgia* with my charred
hands still attached.

Benito had to virtually lift me up the cliff.

26

WE WENT INWARD. I FOLLOWED BENITO, NURSING MY charred wrists. He had to haul me up the last bridges by the slack of my robe. The pain never stopped. The nerves gave no sign of having been cauterized by the red-hot iron. The charred bone broke away; the black flesh split to expose red flesh.

It'll heal, Carpentier.

Oh, *shut up.* And call me Carpenter. Carpentier the Famous Author is dead.

In the empty borderland between the tenth pit and the giants, we sat down. Presently Benito spoke. "Thank you."

"Yeah. I'm sorry I pushed you in."

He didn't say anything. I said, "I thought I had to do it. I thought it was *right.*"

Still nothing. "Look," I said, "I was raised to believe that Benito Mussolini and Adolf Hitler were identical monsters."

Benito sighed. "Sometimes, toward the end, perhaps we were. I didn't start that way. I meant well." He laughed bitterly. "I had good intentions. We know what is said to be paved with those."

"Tell me about it."

He spoke musingly, without looking at me. "After the war I saw my country humiliated. No one believed in anything. Corruption everywhere, laboring people working against wealthy people, middle class working against the government, everyone fighting each other and everyone ruining each other. If they'd only work together—we were Romans, once. We ruled the world. We could be great again, instead of a joke for Clemenceau and Lloyd George to swat aside."

"So you made people work together?"

"I gave Italy hope. For years I even stopped Hitler from taking Austria. Allen, if I'd chosen the side of the Allies in the second war, would I have as great a place in history as Stalin?"

I couldn't say anything to that.

"Yet he killed ten-million peasants. Adolf never equaled that record. As for me, in the early days we used castor oil, not clubs." He sighed. "But you can never stop, once you begin seeing what is better for people than they know themselves. The opposition will make a thorough mess of everything you've done, and you know they will destroy the country. What do you do? Destroy the opposition. Now they really have grievances. Bigger opposition, more police needed to suppress them. But I meant well. I loved my people to the day they killed me."

" 'The purpose of power is power.' "

"*What?*" Benito was badly shocked.

"Never mind. Quote from a novel, *Nineteen Eighty-four*. So then you tried to set up a government here?"

"For my sins, I did." Benito's sudden laugh was like my own howling in the sixth *bolgia:* there was an agonized laugh in him, and it clawed its way through his throat. "Oh, Allen! And you think you've seen Hell! A government among the Evil Counselors— When I tried to get out they stopped me; they needed me as figurehead. Never mind, I got out anyway. I *had* to."

"But you never did anything but good for me. Or anyone else you met, down here."

"How are your hands?"

We looked. Two tiny infant's fists were forming at the lumpy bones of my wrists. "We must wait until they heal. You will never climb with those!" He laughed.

We sat and talked. Hours went by.

"I think the worst was when they shot my cabinet people. Italians shooting men whose only crime was to love Italy and trust me—" He shuddered. "Those are strange scars on your chest."

"I had to play games with the demon in the tenth *bolgia*. Funny, we didn't see him coming back."

"Games?"

Reluctantly I told him. It could have been embarrassing, but it wasn't. He didn't thank me again. Instead he smiled and said, "Do you still believe that Hell is a place of entertainment?"

"No. I didn't even then. I think Geryon convinced me."

"Geryon?"

"Yeah. You may not have noticed, but Geryon is the only nonhuman in Hell who really looks like an ET, an extraterrestrial, something from another world. He's consistent. Not like those patchwork demons, animal traits grafted on a human frame. And when I climbed aboard him I kicked machinery around his waist."

"So?"

I had to laugh. "Oh, *really,* Benito! An antigravity belt? When they've already proved they can take the mass and weight out of anything they like? Geryon was lying. Lying without saying a word."

"And it was Geryon that convinced you? You have seen no proper miracles?"

"I saw one."

I told him where the pitchfork had come from. "That priest climbed the broken bridge in half a ton of gold. He hung from the demon's pitchfork until the demon had to let go, and he *knew* what would happen then."

Benito smiled. "Yes, that was a miracle."

"Too right. I know a miracle when I see one."

"Then you are more fortunate than most of us." He looked thoughtful. "Geryon has looked a little different each time I have seen him."

"That worried me too. Just how often have you made this trip?"

"Six times. Each has been easier for me, although not for the one who accompanied me to the exit. As I told you, it does not matter how many start. Only one leaves."

"And there really is a way out . . . There was a time when I thought you were just leading me into something more horrible. I'm still scared, but not of that."

"Now there remains only the lake of ice. You have nothing to fear."

"I'm afraid to relax. Too often I've thought I was through the worst part."

His look probed my soul. "When the iron began to grow warm in your hands—"

"Tell me all about it."

"I think not. But now there is only the ice. It will be colder than anything you can imagine, but we can endure it. Nothing can bar us now! Soon we reach the center, and then—" He stopped.

"And then?"

"You will see." He looked me in the face. "I think you have enough courage."

"Even now I feel it leaking away. Spit it out, Benito."

"We will meet Lucifer and pass him. Ignore anything he says. When we have passed that, go uphill to Purgatory." He paused. "Without me."

"But you've traveled this route? You know where it leads?"

"No, and yes. I have not traveled it, but I know where it leads."

"How?"

"By faith, and by Dante's description."

"Dante's been wrong a couple of times. Admit it, Benito: you don't know what happened to those six you rescued."

"I know. But I have not seen."

"Do you want to leave Hell? Or are you afraid of what's there?"

"How are your hands?"

They were a child's hands now, still too small to support my weight.

"You didn't answer my question."

"I would leave Hell if I could. I belong here, so long as there are lost souls to be rescued."

"You sent six men and women into the unknown, but you were afraid to go yourself."

He didn't answer, only looked at me.

I stood up. "Come on. My hands'll heal before we need them."

They healed.

We climbed the torso of a chained giant. It was easier than mountain climbing, and harder: mountains don't shake, mountains don't snap at you with teeth the size of medieval shields. We stepped across space from the giant's shoulder to the flat top of a wall. From the wall I watched Benito slide down on the seat of his pants, if he'd been wearing pants. A pity he hadn't found a better way down in six previous trips.

I slid after him.

Imagine one of the Great Lakes frozen over, seen on a moonless night. Maybe it looked like that. I'd never seen any of the Great Lakes. To me it was an ice-skating rink for a society of teleports: big enough to hold, say, one percent of a population of five billion. The wall behind me seemed arrow-straight; the dark ice, infinite.

A breath of a breeze whispered around us and leeched all the warmth from our massless souls. I stiffened with the shock, then crouched down and tried to shelter in my own arms.

Benito was standing. "That will not help. Nothing helps," he said patiently. "You must bear the cold."

If he could do it . . . I stood up and closed my eyes tight against the soft, unreasonably cold breeze. Surely it was below freezing, *way* below freezing. How cold was it? If it could kill a man in minutes, or seconds, I'd never know it. I couldn't die.

"Benito? Burst into flame again for your good friend."

"I would if I could. My apologies, Allen." Benito took my arm. We walked.

It had certainly been worth asking.

Was it water ice we walked on? For all of me, it could have been dry ice, or frozen nitrogen, or something even colder.

I kicked something that cursed me without emotion. I tried to open my eyes. The wind's tears had frozen them shut. I pulled them open, painfully, with my fingers.

"Leave them open," Benito said without pity, "and they will freeze open."

When the urge came to blink I fought it. Then there was no need, for my eyes would not close. I looked back at what I'd kicked. I said, "Sorry."

The face was handsome, photogenic, dignified in middle age, undignified in the way it grimaced and bent to the ice for shelter. Had I seen that face sometime, on television? Maybe. The man was buried to his chin in the ice. At the sound of my voice he cried, "Wait! Are you American?"

"Aren't we all? I can't seem to find anything but."

The head called to another head sitting like a cabbage on the ice. "George! Maybe we can settle this now." It turned back to me. "Late American? Do you know anything about the ABM controversy?"

"Sure. Antiballistic missiles to knock down incoming missiles. The controversy was over whether to build the ABM system."

"Wonderful! All right, sir. George was a Democrat, and I was a Republican. The Democrats were against building the system. The Republicans were in favor of it. But which of us was right?"

"I haven't the faintest idea," I said. "Do you really have nothing better to talk about than that?"

"No!" the man I'd kicked said sharply. "We do not! One of us had to be right! So why are we both here?"

The cold wasn't just getting to me; it had gotten me. I wanted *out,* not conversation. I said, "Other crimes, maybe."

"One of us was wrong," George said. "Senator Gates here thought the system was a waste of money, but he went along with his party. He—"

"It was more than a waste of money! It used up efforts we could have spent on a laser system! Sir,

I've seen how accurate a laser defense system could be against incoming missiles. But politics dictated that I must support the ABM system. I went along."

"I don't know anything about the darned lasers," George said, "except they were highly experimental. Experimental weapons did a lot for the Nazis, didn't they?" He snorted contempt, then sneezed on the freezing air. "I was convinced that the ABM system was needed to defend the country against an atomic attack. But our party platform was in favor of military cutbacks. Officially, so was I."

"Now, sir," Senator Gates said to me, "we can't both have been wrong."

"I think I'm getting the picture. You both *thought* you were wrong."

". . . yes."

"And a mistake could wipe out the United States of America."

Neither answered.

"For what it's worth," I said, "we're still getting Americans in Hell. Corbett died much later than you."

"Thank you," said ex-Senator Gates, and they both turned their faces to the ice again.

"But you were both traitors in your minds."

"Thank you for your help," said ex-Senator George. It was a dismissal.

We walked with care, to avoid kicking heads. There were certainly enough of them. But now it was worse; here the dead had been buried supine, and we would have been stepping on faces.

Once I missed my step and came down hard on a human face. The ice across its eyes crackled under my feet, and I leapt back fast. "Sorry!"

"Thanks," I heard.

"Mistake."

"Thanks, oh, thanks," it said, weeping. "I haven't cried in years. The damned ice froze across my eyes, and I couldn't cry. Thanks."

I felt awful. This was an awful place. "That's okay," I said. I bent and picked the remaining shards of ice from her eyes. "What'd you do?"

"I don't want to say."

"Okay."

I tore the ice visors from a couple of dozen pairs of eyes. Always they froze over again almost immediately. Only one ever said "Thanks." Finally I gave it up. There were just too many.

And the next head I passed screamed, "The ice! Stupid! Tear off the ice! You did it for the others!"

I stopped. "Who're you?"

"None of your business!"

I turned away.

"The ice! Wait! Al Capone, I'm Al Capone! You want names? That's Vito Genovese, trying to turn his face! Wait, I'll show you Lepke! Wait!" He was shouting against a chorus of voices trying to drown him out. I kept walking.

When the noise was behind us Benito said, "I knew Vito Genovese."

"Was he worth talking to?"

"No. Were you thinking of going back? It's cold, Allen."

Sound whispered all around us. Partly it was the breeze, which had stiffened. Partly it was the chattering of teeth. I'd suppressed that reflex in myself; it wasn't warming me at all.

But in all that expanse of ice, there was only one point of motion. I caught it in the corner of my eye, way off to one side. Doubted my senses. Kept looking. Saw it again.

"Benito?" I pointed.

He found it. "I had no idea. I thought I was the only one."

"You may be. It seems to be one man. And a dog."

They had noticed us, and they angled to meet us. As they came closer I saw my mistake. The dog was a lizard, its scarlet color leeched from it by the cold. And the man was the black-bearded thief who had stolen my shape at the seventh pit.

We studied each other. No greeting seemed appropriate. Finally I gestured and said, "Benito Mussolini. I'm Allen Carpenter."

"Jesse James. This lizard is Bob Ford."

"What was that all about, that business there at the bridge?"

"A bunch of us got together," said Jesse. "We thought maybe we could cooperate in getting one of us out. It turned out a man couldn't throw a lizard far enough. But we could stand a human pyramid against one of the walls, and the top man could throw a lizard at the bridge. I was the lizard."

"Funny nobody thought of it before."

He sighed. "It's getting those animals to work together, that's the problem. All the time we were trying to make the pyramid, some of us in the lizard form kept biting the ones in human form. We didn't get anything done till we had a dozen big lizards to guard us while we made the pyramid."

"Figures. Why'd you jump back?"

"I had to tell them which way was out."

"You might not have got out again. They might not even have let you take human form again."

He nodded.

I remembered something. A line from a song. "It was little Robert Ford, that dirty little coward, I wonder how does he feel, for he ate of Jesse's bread, and he slept in Jesse's bed, and he laid Jesse James in his grave . . ." "Bob Ford. Didn't he kill you? Shot you while you were taking a bath?"

"Hanging a picture. Yeah, he shot me, all right. I was following your advice—for which I thank you, stranger." He laughed. "And there was Bob Ford's head sitting on the ice. I thought it over for a while. I wandered around and around him, wondering what I could do to him, and wondering if I still hated him." The lizard was rubbing affectionately against his leg. "I finally bit him on the nose."

It hit me like a stiff shot of good whiskey. "You can get out of the ice!"

"Sure, friend. I just reached into that man-shaped bubble and picked up a lizard. Well, which way now?"

"Inward," Benito said. "Let us go. It is cold here."

That had to be the most unnecessary statement of all time. We moved inward, and the wind came up. It was blowing right in our faces. Pretty soon it was a real howler, as bad as the circle of the winds. I wondered if Corbett had ever got back there . . .

The wind whistled past us and lifted Jesse off the ice. The lizard squealed and leaped after him, and the wind caught it too. Man and lizard were bowled end over end across the ice, then lifted and flung high and outward. I watched them dwindle.

"So close," I said. "They were so close!"

"They were not ready," Benito said. "Perhaps they must see what is done to others. Theft and treachery may not have been all they did. It is even possible that they will be blown all the way back to the Vestibule and must make their way back. Come."

"But—"

"They know the way, Allen. Come!"

"All right." We bowed our heads against the wind and staggered on. The wind had been entirely too selective for coincidence. It had thrown Jesse and Ford an unguessable distance without knocking me or Benito off our feet. I thought it was a good omen . . . for us.

27

SUDDENLY THERE WERE NO MORE HEADS. THERE WAS only the ice, and the wind that had blown the others away. We leaned into it and kept moving.

I said, "Hell has run out of sins?"

"Look down."

Hell had not run out of sinners. They were buried beneath the ice in weird positions. Once I looked down, and then no more.

We walked crouched, wrapped in our own arms, to no purpose. The wind had early sucked every erg of heat out of us.

I saw motion ahead, high up.

As we drew near a shadowy mass loomed around the suggestion of motion. Pterodactyls on a mountain? Restless, rhythmic motion, like the wings of enormous birds. And gradually it all came clear.

There was a humanoid form, a hairy torso more than a mile tall. We stood at the bottom, at waist level, and looked up at three vast faces whose features were almost lost in distance. Bat wings flapped on either side of each face, and the wind was now beating down at our heads.

This was a very different picture from the dapper gentleman who offers to buy your soul. Or from Milton's epic hero, proud and unrepentant. One could not imagine playing riddles or chess games with this hideous, miserable, helpless mountain. I studied it almost without fear.

All three pairs of jaws were moving in the same rhythm as the wings. Something fluttered around the lips . . .

"Benito, what's he chewing on?"

"Are you sure you want to know?"

"Skip it. Which way is out? *Hey*—" I reached to stop him, not fast enough. Benito was striding straight toward Lucifer.

He stopped at the edge of the ice.

The ice ended short of Lucifer himself. There was three feet of empty space all around the enormous waist.

And no navel. I couldn't have missed it. It would have been big enough to hide a battleship.

"You must climb down," said Benito.

I looked into the gap. "After you."

He shook his head. "I cannot leave. There are others to rescue."

"I don't go without you."

"You have not shown such fear before."

"It's not all fear. You've rescued seven of us, now rescue yourself. You've earned it. If this doesn't lead to where you think it does, we can help each other get back."

"What if I turn back now, leaving you here?"

I'd wondered about that myself. "I don't know, and that's the truth. But there's a moral problem. You're a better man than I am—"

He smiled sardonically. "I? The murderous dictator you pushed into the eighth pit?"

"You've changed since you reached Hell. You've given *me* no evil counsel. I guess that's the point. If you haven't changed in Hell, if you haven't earned the right to leave, then I haven't and won't. If you can't go, I can't."

"I, I think I can go. I choose not to."

"If you can leave Hell, you'll have to prove it."

He studied my face . . . and then he smiled a joyful, luminous smile. He turned and stepped across the gap and had two fistfuls of coarse hair. And a sound beat down at our heads, a wind with an almost subsonic voice in it.

"Carpentier."

I looked straight up. Lucifer's middle face was looking down the curve of Lucifer's chest. Two fluttering human legs protruded like a ghastly cigarette from the corner of the mouth. It spoke, and the deep bass voice blew down to me.

"What will you tell God when you see Him?"

I didn't answer.

"Will you tell Him that He could learn morality from Vlad the Impaler?"

Benito was far below, clinging like a tick in the billowing hair, waiting for me. I stepped across and worked my way down. As I did, my weight seemed to increase, against all the laws of physics. It scared me. I was back in Infernoland, climbing down into the quantum black hole Big Juju had used for artificial gravity . . .

Benito looked up at me curiously. "What did he say to you?"

I shook my head.

We descended, getting heavier. There was a point

where I must have weighed tons, and all of it pushing inward toward my navel. No quantum black hole
crushed and swallowed me. I hadn't really expected
one. Benito worked his way around until his feet
pointed at me, and kept climbing. I followed his ex-
ample.

Now we climbed up. Once I found breath to laugh
at the picture we would have made: two men climbing
at least half a mile of hairy leg, like ticks in the Devil's
hair. I half-expected to pass a dong the size of the
Empire State Building, testicles like twin Astrodomes.
There was nothing but hair.

The climb seemed endless, but it ended, not in
ice but in an echoing grotto of gray rock, dimly lit.
The Devil's hooves still loomed over us, big enough
to stamp a city flat.

We lay on our backs on the smooth rock, panting.
Somewhere a running stream made a bright, happy
gurgling sound. The dim light came from a single
bright pinpoint source overhead. The rock curved inward over our heads, but it never closed. It stretched
away like the neck of an inverted funnel, straight up
for an unguessable distance.

Presently I got up and found the stream and drank
from it. The water was clear and sweet. There is the
peace of deep sleep, and once I had thought there
would be peace in death. I drank again, then lay
with my fingers trailing in the water. Peace in death:
I'd found it.

But Benito was on his feet. "Onward!" he cried,
and began to climb. The handholds were not difficult,
and he moved like a spider monkey, or like a fat
man who no longer weighs anything at all.

He looked down from the inward-tilting gray slope
of grotto roof. "A four-thousand-mile climb, if Dante

was half right!" he bellowed cheerfully. "Are you coming?"

"I'm afraid not."

"What did you say?"

"No!"

I sighed in exasperation when I saw him climbing back down, but I'd half-expected it. He dropped the last few feet, and it did seem he fell like a settling balloon, too slowly. "What was it Satan said to you?"

"He asked me what I would say to God."

"Well?"

"I have to know something before I can speak to God at all."

Benito waited.

"I have to know the purpose of Hell."

"Come and ask Him!"

"You don't get it. Every torture in Hell was too much too late. Punishment? But it's *infinite* punishment for things that are *little* in comparison. Dracula caused a lot of people a lot of pain and death, but it *ended*. George only lied to people to make them buy things! And what about the fat lady in the Vestibule area?

"What's the *point?* To teach us a lesson? But we're *dead*. Revenge, punishment? Completely out of proportion. Balance? Does the universe need as much pain in it as pleasure? I couldn't *take* Heaven if that was the case."

"There is a reason, and the reason is good. I *know*."

"Yeah? I don't. There's only one *possible* excuse for Hell, and I almost missed it in the ravings of a crazy psychiatrist. It has to be the final training ground. If nothing can get a soul into Heaven in its *life,* there's still Hell, God's last attempt to get his attention. Like a catatonic in a hotbox, like me in that bottle, if Hell won't make a man yell for help, then it was still worth a try."

Benito was nodding. "You may be right. You may have found the purpose of Hell."

"Yeah. Yeah, but do you see where it leaves me? *Everyone* in Hell has to be able to leave once he's learned enough about himself. *Everyone,* even the trees in the Wood of the Suicides, even the poor devils in the boiling pitch and the sullen types anchored under the lake. Even the ones who think they're satisfied, the ones in the First Circle. And I can't leave Hell until I'm sure they can do it."

Benito nodded. "We go back."

"No, no, you idiot!" I was furious. "How can I tell anyone he can leave unless I know you did it? You're going up! And I'm going to watch you do it!"

He thundered, "Carpenter, you must still learn humility!"

"Granted. And you?"

"But they need me. They . . . ah. They have you."

"They have me." I put out my hand. "Good-bye, Benito. Good luck. I hope you find—"

He stepped past my hand and wrapped his arms around me and squeezed all the air out of me. I said something like, "Huff!", and hugged him back. We held the embrace for a long moment. Then Benito released me and turned away fast—I couldn't see his face—and started climbing.

I lay flat on the rock and looked up. At the end of the vertical tube, the pinpoint light source had all but vanished, leaving Benito nearly invisible. Many hours later the light brightened again, and I knew I was seeing the sun. Benito was a dark fleck that moved if I watched it long enough.

He had made good progress before the light dimmed and went out.

The water sounds burbled back from the rock walls. I lay with my arms folded behind my head, taking joy in laziness. The peace of this place was almost tangible. Worrying seemed inappropriate here: a breach of good manners.

What did they do to Billy? Did the priest get out all right? How could any thinking being do such a thing to Mrs. Herrnstein? I've got to get back—

But I felt no sense of urgency. The damned had all the time there was, and so did I. Hell was the violent ward of a hospital for the theologically insane. Some could be cured.

I would have to return to Hell. I was afraid of that; not afraid of the pains, or that the demons would catch me, because the pains would heal, and pain in the right cause is a badge of honor. As to the demons, there'd be no chance they could hold me. Not now. I knew.

No. My fear was of the doubts that would return. They would come, and I'd just have to live with them, and fight them with my memory of these few moments of peace. There were no doubts here. None at all.

The light was back, and there was a tiny mote in it that moved even as I watched. My eyes were better than human now; else I'd never have seen him at all.

The light was dimming with sunset when the mote moved out of it and left it clear.

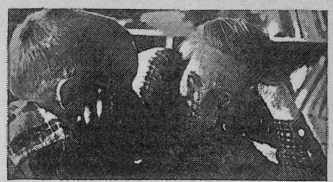

Today they're playing word games.
Before he's five, he can be reading 150 words a minute.

HOW TO GIVE YOUR CHILD A SUPERIOR MIND

A remarkable new book tells how you, yourself—at home—with no special training can actually add as much as thirty points to your child's effective I.Q....how you can help him move ahead quickly in school and enable him to be more successful in an education-conscious world.

Best of all, your child can achieve this early success without being pushed and without interference with a happy, normal, well-adjusted childhood.

GIVE YOUR CHILD A SUPERIOR MIND provides a planned program of home instruction that any parent can start using immediately. *You will learn:*

1. How to awaken your child's inborn desire to learn.
2. How to teach your child to read.
3. How to help your child streak ahead in math.
4. How to give your child the power of abstract reasoning.
5. How to increase your child's effective I.Q.

At all bookstores, or mail coupon today.

YOGA
FOR ALL AGES

Relax wound up nerves and muscles. Maintain youthful vitality and looks. And do it all in just a few minutes a day—with the world's fastest-growing way to physical well-being.

Fitness for the whole family

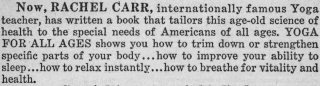

Now, **RACHEL CARR**, internationally famous Yoga teacher, has written a book that tailors this age-old science of health to the special needs of Americans of all ages. YOGA FOR ALL AGES shows you how to trim down or strengthen specific parts of your body...how to improve your ability to sleep...how to relax instantly...how to breathe for vitality and health.

Special features of this book:

—**Rachel Carr's Six-Week Yoga Course.** Acquire a basic mastery of physical yoga to help keep you fit for the rest of your life.

—**Yoga exercises you can do in a chair.** Ideal for office workers, old people, and the handicapped.

—**Yoga for children.** The Rooster, The Cobra, The Swan and other exercises which children find great fun.

—**Simple steps in relaxing.**

—**Concentration and Meditation.** An introduction to the mental and spiritual aspects of yoga.

—**Lavishly illustrated** with more than 250 step-by-step photographs and drawings.

At your bookstore or mail this NO RISK coupon

SIMON AND SCHUSTER, DEPT. 67, 630 5th Ave.
New York, New York 10020

Please send me Rachel Carr's YOGA FOR ALL AGES. If I am not completely delighted with this book, I may return it within 10 days and owe nothing. Otherwise, I'll send only $8.95 plus mailing costs as payment in full. (Please Print)

Name_____

Address_____

City_____State_____Zip_____

☐ SAVE. Enclose $8.95 now and publisher pays mailing costs. Same 10-day privilege with full refund guaranteed.

S 81/3